ALICE IN PLUNDERLAND

Alice in Plunderland

Steve McCaffery

Illustrations by
Clelia Scala

BookThug · 2015
Department of Narrative Studies

FIRST EDITION

Canada Council
for the Arts

Conseil des Arts
du Canada

ONTARIO ARTS COUNCIL
CONSEIL DES ARTS DE L'ONTARIO
an Ontario government agency
un organisme du gouvernement de l'Ontario

The production of this book was made possible through the generous
assistance of the Canada Council for the Arts and the Ontario Arts Council.

LIBRARY AND ARCHIVES CANADA
CATALOGUING IN PUBLICATION

McCaffery, Steve, author
    Alice in Plunderland / Steve McCaffery ; Clelia Scala, illustrator.

(Department of narrative studies)
Issued in print and electronic formats.
ISBN 978-1-77166-089-1 (PBK.).--ISBN 978-1-77166-110-2 (HTML)

    1. Carroll, Lewis, 1832-1898--Adaptations. I. Scala, Clelia,
illustrator II. Title. III. Series: Department of narrative studies

PS8575.C33A45 2015   C813'.54   C2015-900405-5
                                          C2015-900406-3

PRINTED IN CANADA

Table of Contents

All in the golden afternoon
Stoned to the max we slushed
Around for syringes, that with skill
Into our veins we pushed
While little hands held little pills
And drugs were seldom flushed.

Ah cruel Junk! In such an hour
Within our junky bones
To beg a tale of death too weak
To cut the finest tones!
Yet what can one poor junky do
When feening with the moans?

Thus grew the tale of Plunderland
Thus slowly, pill by pill
It brought on junky dreams and then
Cold turkey 'gainst our will,
Shaking punctured arms and legs
Yet still existing: still.

CHAPTER I.

Down the Man-Hole

Alice was desperately coke-broke and beginning to find life a bit of a drag standing in line with her dumb-ass sister in the local branch of BMO, faced with the bleak reality of being clean out of lettuce to score even a couple of lines of king's habit: once or twice she had peeped into the open bank book her sister was checking, but it had zilch deposits or withdrawals in it, "and what the fu** use is a sister's bank book," thought Alice, "without any moolah in it to borrow?"

So she was considering in her own mind (as well as she could, for the combination of the hot day and opium suppositories made her feel very sleepy and stupid), whether a visit to the ATM outside the bank would be worth the trouble of trying to get some emergency cash by keying in her dear mama's PIN, when suddenly a young bank teller with shocking pink hair ran close by her.

There was nothing so *very* remarkable in that; nor did Alice think it so *very* much out of the way to hear the teller say to herself, "Oh pshit! Oh pshit! I shall be late!" (when she thought it over afterwards, it occurred to her that she ought to have wondered at this, but at the time it all seemed quite natural); but when the teller actually *took a wad of hundred-dollar bills* out of her purse, and kissed it, and then hurried on, Alice turned around, for it flashed across her mind that she had never before seen a bank teller with a fat wad of C-notes and kissing it so ardently, at that. So, burning with curiosity and the authentic thought of effectively mugging her, she ran across the street after her, and fortunately was just in time to see the teller fall into a large open man-hole down and down under the pavement.

Laughter, as well we know, is a temporary convulsion of the nerves; and it seems as if nature cuts short the rapid thrill of pleasure on the nerves by a sudden convulsion of them, to prevent the sensation becoming painful, and in another moment (after she'd stopped laughing that is) down went Alice after the teller, never once considering how in the world she was to get out again. The man-hole connected to the city sewer system for some way, and then turned to the left so suddenly that Alice had not a moment to think about stopping herself before she found herself crawling through the slime and pshit of the main sewer system.

Sewage, children, is a highly complex liquid; a large proportion of its most offensive matter is, of course, human excrement discharged from water closets, and also urine thrown down gully holes. But mixed with this is the water from kitchens containing vegetable, animal, and other refuse as well as that from wash houses containing soap. There is also the drainage from stables and discotheques and cow houses of child prostitution, as well as the fetal remains from abortion clinics and slaughter-houses containing human, animal, and vegetable offal. Either the sewage was very deep, or Alice moved very slowly, for she had ample time as she crawled along to check out the insalubrious landscape about her and to wonder what the f*ck was going to happen next. First, she swallowed a couple of leapers that magically materialized and then tried to look down and make out what she was coming to, but it was too dark to see anything and noxious fumes clouded the entire system; then, with the aid of her cigarette lighter, she looked at the sides of the tunnel and noticed that they were caked in dried fecal matter and well-executed, tag-gang graffiti; here and there she saw rats and enormous cockroaches and one or two down-and-out Vietnam veteran amputees crawling along against the walls. She picked up a plastic bag from one of the elevated sewer ramps as she passed; it was labeled "HIGH-GRADE COCAINE." To her great disappointment it was almost empty: however, she snorted the bit of snow remaining but did not like to hang on to the bag for fear of being found in possession of an illicit substance and was well aware that the Federal Drug Enforcement Agency, as well as the FBI and RCMP, frequently investigated North American city sewer systems for stashes of hidden drugs. Accordingly, she concealed it on the edge of a storm overflow, carefully wiping off her fingerprints as she waded on past it.

"Holy pshyt!" expleted Alice to herself, "after crawling through raw sewage like this, it'll be a piece of cake to dumpster dive in the pharmaceutical garbage and hazmat at the local hospitals! How supercool they'll all think me at home! Why, I wouldn't say a thing about it, even if I fell off the top of the f***ing house!" (Which was very likely to take place.)

Crawl, crawl, crawl. Would the snail-paced perambulation through the egg-shaped sewer *never* come to an end? "I wonder how many kilometres I've crawled by this time?" she said aloud. "Holy crap, it sure as hell stinks down here, I must be getting somewhere near the centre of Tronna. Let me see: that would be 3.7 kilometres south from where I fell, I think—" (for, you see, Alice had learnt several things of this sort in her lessons at the exclusive Bishop Strachan School for Girls situated on Lonsdale Avenue, and though this was not a *very* auspicious opportunity for showing off her knowledge of topology, as there was no one to listen to her, still it was good practice to say it over) "—yes, that's about the right distance— but then I wonder what Latitude or Longitude I've got to?" (Alice had no idea what Latitude was, or Longitude either, but thought they, like methylenedioxymethamphetamine and supercalifragilisticexpialidocious, were nice grand words to say and even grander drugs to consume.)

Presently she recommenced her monologue. "I wonder if

I shall crawl all the way from Bloor Street West, Tronna, to Long Island! How funny it'll seem to come out in that wealthy American county over there among the affluent dinosaurs and dabblers who walk each afternoon with their designer-clipped poodles in Eisenhower Park! Nissan County, I think it's called—" (she was rather glad there was no one listening this time, as it didn't sound at all the right name of the county) "—but I shall have to ask them what the name of the frigging county is, you know. Please, Ma'am, is this Nissan or Suffolk?" (And she tried to curtsy knee-deep in the sewage as she spoke—fancy *curtsying* to the Governor General of Canada as you're crawling through raw sewage! Do you think you could manage it?) "And what an ignorant little girl she'll think me for asking! No, it'll never do to ask: perhaps I shall see it written up somewhere."

Crawl, crawl, crawl. She had downed her final leaper and her chequebook was at zilch and there was nothing else to do, so after a cogibundance of disjunctive reflections, Alice soon began talking to herself again. "Siegfried will miss me very much to-night, I should think!" (Siegfried was her cheating accountant who worked for the Bonadio Group and who was destined to invent a line of defensive forts in 1916 and have the line named after him.) "I hope my parents remember to pay his exorbitant house-call fee and charge me a penalty for no-show at tea time. Siegfried, my dear! I wish you were down here with me! There are no tax returns to fill out for your exorbitant fee I'm afraid, but you might catch an enormous rat (exactly like yourself), and that's very like one of those small alligators that people flush down the toilet when they've grown too big to be kept as pets, you know. But do small alligators eat rats, I wonder?" And here Alice began to get rather torpid (no doubt owing to the effects of the white powder blending with the toxic sewage fumes), and went on saying to herself, in a dreamy sort of way, "Do small alligators eat large rats? Do

small alligators eat large rats?" and sometimes, "Do large rats
eat small alligators?" for, you see, as she couldn't answer either
question, it didn't much matter which way she put it. She felt
that she was dozing off, and had just begun to dream that she
was walking hand in hand with Ulysses Simpson Grant, and
saying to the dead president very earnestly, "Now, Mr. Dead
President, tell me the truth: have you ever literally eaten a rat?
I know they sometimes turn up on Chinese take-out menus
advertised as Ginger Chicken stir-fry," when suddenly, thump!
thump! down she tripped on a Merryweather-patented fixed
hydraulic sewage flusher, and fell upon a hard heap of sewage
and waste cans, and the crawling was over.

Her Grail Quest through the enteric realm was finally at
an end. Alice was not a bit hurt, and she jumped up on to her
feet in a moment: she looked up, but it was all dark overhead;
before her was another long passage, but this time sewage-free
and the young bank teller was still in sight, hurrying down it
with her shocking-pink hair and thick wad of hundred-dollar
bills forming an aesthetically pleasing chromatic contrast.
After her unpropitious odyssey through the cloacal catacombs
of Tronna, there was not a moment to be lost: disregarding the
insalubrious topography, away went Alice as fast as a fart in a
wind tunnel, and was just in time to hear the teller lament, as
she turned a corner, "Holy pshitt, I've got to get this scratch to
Jimmy quick!" She was close behind her when she turned the
corner, but the shocking-pink-haired teller was no longer to be
seen: Alice found herself in a long, low, dingy alley, which was
illuminated by a row of homemade oil lamps hanging from the
walls and the whole scene reeking of stale piss. "Oh, too cool,
this must be the genuine underworld of thieves, gangsters,
hookers, and drug addicts," ululated a jubilant Alice to herself.
There were doors all along the alley, all heavily padlocked
and tagged with urban graffiti (mainly Wildstyle, with some
Bubble Letters and a few highly impressive Fat Cap motifs

signed "Deadboy"); and when Alice had been all the way down
one side and up the other, trying every door, she ambulated
with profound despondence down the middle, kicking at the
empty Molson Canadian and Labatt 50 cans that confected
the terrain, and glancing around at the admittedly awesome
graffiti, wondering where the fu** she would find a toilet she
could use (by this time she needed badly to micturate), and
how she was ever to get out again.

Suddenly she came upon an unmarked wooden crate,
constructed out of solid pine; there was nothing on it except a
crack kit with some back door that Alice quickly polished off,
a few dozen cigarette butts, razor blades, crack suppositories,
a couple of broken chillums, and what looked like a house key.
Alice's primary thought was that it might belong to one of the
padlocked portals in the alley; but, no way! either the locks
were too large, or the key was too small, but at any rate the
incompatible dimensions of the projectile and the intended
metallic recipient precluded the possibility of opening any of
them. However, on the second time round, she came upon a
trash can she had not noticed before, and behind it was a little
door about eighteen inches high: she tried the key in the lock,
and to her great delight it fitted!

Alice opened the door and found that it led into a small
passage, not much larger than an escape tunnel from a
government safe-house: she knelt down and looked along
the passage into the coolest garden you ever saw. Through a
lambent haze she could ascertain that it was amply equipped
with the most majestic and thriving marijuana plants, an in-
ground Ameri-Brand custom-made kidney-shaped swimming
pool constructed out of the finest fibreglass that came with a
lifetime guarantee, complete with a dozen or so Swimline blue
fabric-covered U-Seat inflatable happy chairs and innumerable
duck toys, artificial palm trees, and an awesome poolside bar!
How she longed to get far away from that nasty, dark sewer

system, and circumgyrate among those bright bottles of vodka, tequila, and white rum, among those kind of beautiful girls in bikinis and sunglasses that you see only in James Bond films, each reclining on a deluxe Body Love dual lounger with a cocktail in one hand and a coke spoon in the other, but she could not even get her head through the doorway; "and even if my head would go through," thought poor, stoned Alice, "it would be of f**k all use without my shoulders. Some frigging security system here! Oh man, I wish I could diminish my stature to about the size of two ounces of monkey dribble! I think I could, if I only knew how to begin." For, you see, so many out-of-the-way things had happened lately that Alice had begun to think, like Leonardo da Vinci and Albert Einstein had before her, that very few things indeed were really impossible.

There seemed to be little use in waiting by the little door, so she went back to the wooden crate, half hoping she might find a freshly rolled mooster on it, or at any rate a morning wake-up or a modicum of lamb's bread: this time, however, she found a small bottle standing on it ("which certainly was not here before," affirmed Alice), and round the neck of the bottle was a paper label, with the words "DRINK ME" beautifully printed on it in large, blue, Trebuchet letters.

It was all very well to say "Drink me" in beautifully printed large, blue, Trebuchet letters, but the wise little crackhead Alice was not going to do *that* in a hurry. "No way José, I'll look first," she mumbled inarticulately, "and see whether it's marked *'poison'* or not;" for despite her aquatic propensities she still had sufficient remaining brain cells to remember having read several nice little histories about rich, spoiled, child bingers who had got burnt by bad business ventures, such as Ponzi schemes and other unpleasant things, all because they needed some quick lettuce for their habit and they *would* not remember the simple fact that all financiers are crooks and are out for nothing but their own profit: such as that Chief Executive Officer at a bank in Cincinnati who gave himself a five million dollar Christmas bonus after having his bank bailed out by the federal government to the tune of 13 billion dollars. (Such things never happened in Canada.) She had also never forgotten from her kindergarten chemistry classes that if you drink much from a bottle marked "poison," it is almost certain to disagree with you, sooner or later.

However, this bottle was *not* marked "poison," so Alice, being something of a cabbage head, ventured to pour some down her most aqueous and irriguous esophagus, and noting the label said "98% PROOF" and finding it very bomb diggity (it had, in fact, a sort of mixed flavour of cherry liqueur, pineapple daiquiri, toffee-flavoured vodka, gin, vermouth, and just a subtle hint of coconut and pomegranate), she very soon finished it off.

*   *   *   *   *   *

*   *   *   *   *

*   *   *   *   *   *

"What a phucking phabulous pheeling!" alliterated Alice euphemistically and exceedingly intoxicated; "that liquor sure packs one inferno of a punch! I must be as drunk as a skunk in a trunk." And so she was indeed: she was now finding it difficult to stand, and her face brightened at the thought that she was now in a state of intoxication sufficient to drive impaired straight through the little door into that lovely garden with its fantastic poolside bar. First, however, she waited for a few minutes and delayed her trajectory until she'd completed a rainbow yawn into the sewer system: she felt a thankful relief after she'd fully thrown up. "I should try to stay sober I suppose," she surmised, "like my therapist advises, otherwise I might end, you know," murmured Alice to herself, "crashing out wired and getting mugged and all my money and ID heisted, and maybe even stripped naked and left in an alley for dead. I wonder what that should be like then?" And she tried to fancy what it would be like to be mugged, stripped naked and dumped in an alley, for she could not remember ever having seen such a thing except on cable television.

After a while, finding that nothing more happened, she decided to effect her entry without delay into the garden with the fabulous kidney-shaped swimming pool and the even more fabulous poolside bar; but, alas for poor Alice! when she got to the door, she discovered she had forgotten the house key, and when she stumbled back to the crate for it, she found herself so tanked-up there was no way she could reach it: she could see it quite plainly through her bleary eyes, and she tried her best to stagger along the ground and pull herself up one of the sides of the crate, but was too plastered by now to do so; and when she had tired herself out with trying, the poor little thing collapsed in a heap and hiccupped.

"Come, there's no use in hiccupping like that!" muttered the extremely tipsy Alice in a semblance of communication to herself, having been prostrated due to the excess of the potent liquor she had consumed and its concomitant dissipation. Rather slurring her words, "I advise you to leave off this minute!" She generally gave herself very sound advice (though she very seldom followed it), and sometimes she drank herself so unconscious as to wake up not knowing who or where the f**k she was. Once, after a full deck of crystals, she remembered trying to punch her own face for having cheated in a game of imaginary high-stakes poker she was playing against herself, for this curious child was paranoid-schizophrenic as well as being majorly up against the stem, and very fond of pretending to be two people. "But it's no use now," concluded poor Alice, pissed as an alligator, "to pretend to be two people! Why, there's sufficient enough of me left sober to make one respectable person!"

Even in this state Alice could recall that drugs are at the heart of the new imperialism and soon her blurry eyes fell on a triple-fold that was lying beside the crate: she opened it, and found in it several grams of white powder with an accompanying note, on which the words "SNORT ME" were beautifully marked in lurid red nail polish (or it might have been human blood!) "What the pshitte, I'll do what it says and snort it through this tooter," decided Alice hiccuping, "that is, if I can find my frigging nose. I do hope it's cocaine, which is generally considered to be the caviar of street drugs. If it gets me coasting again, I might be able to reach the key; and if it proves to be a bummer and brings on the cocaine blues and I start to see coke bugs nibbling through my skin, or if it brings on a nightmare hallucination in which I creep under the door away from a pack of blue devils headed by Sandie Rinaldo or Don Cherry, either way I'll get into the poolside bar, and I don't care a pshytt what happens!"

She inhaled at first about two abes-worth of the schoolcraft, and then quickly a good deal more with all the subdued relish of an epicure, and said to herself in a highly hyperactive manner, "Which way? Which f*ckin* way?" holding her hand on the top of her head to feel which way it was growing, and she was quite surprised to find that she remained the same size: to be sure, this generally happens when one toots a lot of devil's dandruff, but Alice had got so much into the way of expecting nothing but out-of-the-way things to happen, that it seemed (as it did to Hermann Goering, John Belushi, William S. Burroughs, Drew Barrymore, Tila Tequila, David Hasselhoff, Robert Downey Jr., Farrah Fawcett, Charlie Sheen, Pope Pius III, Johnny Depp, Jamie Lee Curtis, Marilyn Monroe, Elizabeth Taylor, and other legendary tweakers) pshit-dull and stupid for life to go on in the common way.

So she set to work, and eftsoons finished off the contents

· of the entire triple-fold and felt quite at home as she thought of all the famous celebrities, fashion models, high-ranking politicians, Tronna mayors, and Wall Street traders who use blow just like her.

       *   *   *   *   *   *

          *   *   *   *   *

       *   *   *   *   *   *

CHAPTER II.

The Pool of Wet Dreams

"Wasted and more wasted!" averred Alice (she was now so chalked-up from blowout, that for the moment she was quite incapable of speaking good English); "now I'm feeling as if I'm as turned on as the first monkey launched into space! Goodbye, gee, man, I'm whacky a-boot to the max!" (for when she looked down at her feet through her now enormously dilated pupils, they seemed to be tiny moving colonies of ants, she was getting so charged up by the c-dust). "Oh, my poor little ants, I wonder who will feed you now, dears? I'm sure *I* shan't be able, with my increased blood pressure, constricted peripheral blood vessels, increasing abdominal pain and general nausea! I shall be a great deal too baked to trouble myself about you poor little assholes: you must manage the best way you can—but I must be kind to them," cogitated Alice, "or perhaps they won't crawl the way I want them to crawl into my sister's underwear! Let me see: I'll give them a pony pack of cactus buttons for Christmas."

And the stupid, blasted little Alice went on planning to herself how she would manage it. "They'll have to go via a carrier to a broker," she reasoned; "maybe a low-key dinosaur in Downsview, or a runner who knows the route and how weird and crazy it'll seem, sending cactus buttons to one's own colonies of pet ants! And how crazy the directions will look!

> *Alice's moving ant colonies, esq.*
> *Diabolitos,*
> · *near the fender,*
> *(with Alice's love).*

Oh dear, what sweet, f*ck*ng nonsense I'm talking!" She giggled before swallowing a couple of amyl nitrites conveniently present on the crate.

Just then (and not surprisingly) she slipped on a banana skin and her head struck against the edge of the crate: in fact she was now totally high, and she at once took up the house key and staggered in the approximate direction of the garden door. Poor, baked Alice! It was as much as she could do, lying down on one side, to look through into the garden with one bleary eye and a dumb smile tattooed onto her visage; but to get through was more hopeless than ever: she sat upright (with difficulty) and began to use again.

"You ought to be ashamed of yourself," remarked Alice to herself, in profound self-remonstration "a great, unrepentant crackhead like you" (there was indeed veracity in this claim), "to go on using in this way—and so young! Stop this moment, I tell you! It's bad for the heart, lungs, brain, and for the blood vessels, and it can lead to severe and unpredictable aggression and morbid depression." But she continued on all the same, sniffed a little locker room, then started shedding gallons of sweat until there was a large pool all round her, about four inches deep and reaching halfway down the hall, creating quite a glaucous atmosphere. But Alice was so all-lit-up by now that she couldn't tell her perspiration from the raw sewage through which she had peregrinated.

After a time she heard a little pattering of feet in the distance, and she hastily dried herself to see who or what was coming. It was the young bank teller with the shocking-pink hair returning, splendidly inked in elevated-mind-style tattoos and most alluringly damascened in a tight emerald-green leather jacket with matching niger kid gloves over a low-cut sleeveless, beige, spandex top (slightly lighter than her skin) complete with an african woodbine in one hand and a big 8 of g-rock in the other: she came along the alley in a great hurry, obviously riding the wave and muttering to herself as she came, "Oh pshit! Jimmy! Jimmy! Oh! won't he be majorly pissed off when he finds out I've been boosting from his stash!" Alice felt so desperate for some galloping horse, or even a roll of bamba to feed her need, that she was ready to ask help of the first bag bride she met; so, when the teller came near her, she began in a low, timid voice, "Hey excuse me Miss, I need to score badly but I'm broke. Can you shoot me an abe of bad rock as a freebie? If you don't mind—you look the generous kind." The bank teller started violently, dropped the african woodbine, but hung on to the g-rock and scurried away into the darkness as hard as she could go. It turned out that the young teller with shocking-pink hair was actually a hardened hooker named Samantha who had stolen the drugs from her pimp, Jimmy the Switch, after turning over her night's earnings to him in the front seat of his 1982 Cadillac Eldorado parked in a location unknown to this narrator.

Alice took up the afghani indica and toked up immediately. As this part of the underworld was very hot from the fires

lit in the burning trash cans by derelicts, meth heads and subterranean scum of that ilk, she kept fanning herself all the time with a folded copy of the *Globe and Mail* she had brought with her through the sewer system (in case, no doubt, she found the opportunity to do the crossword puzzle) and went on yakking to herself: "Dear, dear! How screwed up everything is to-day! And yesterday things went on just as usual. I wonder if I've been ripped off during the night? Let me think: was I totally spent when I got up this morning? I almost think I can remember feeling I was. But if I'm not the same, the next question is, who am I? Ah, *that's* the great puzzle for a crackhead!" And she commenced cogitating in an existential fashion over all the children she knew that were of the same age as her and addicts like herself, to see if she could have been changed for any of them in this most magical of narratives.

"I'm sure I'm not Ada," she mumbled, "for Ada's nipples are pierced and she's tattooed all the way down one side of her body and leg in a fetching pre-colonial pointillist style, reminiscent of ancient Maori tribal patterns. Besides, she only has an ice cream habit, plus the odd pharming ventures, and the only merchandise that she shoots occasionally are delatestryl and hail." And I'm sure I can't be Mabel, she's a fu*k*d-up acid freak from a Scarborough housing estate and besides, I know all sorts of things, and she, oh! she knows f*** all. That bitch doesn't know the difference between half moons and half tracks! Besides, she's she, and I'm I, and—oh dear, how puzzling it all is when you're on a trip! I'll try if I know all the things I used to know. Let me see: one ounce of crack is called a karachi; 20–30% pure pangonadlot is called detroit pink; and one to 15 ounces of heroin is called a devil's dick! Oh, what the pshitt, I shall never get to a zombie and a zoomer at this rate! But let's keep going. Zip is the name for crystal methamphetamine, and waffle dust comes from lysergic acid diethylamide, and dead president is the name of an injectable steroid—no, *that's* all wrong, I'm certain! I must have been changed for that cretin Mabel! I'll try and say "How doth the little—" and she crossed her hands on her lap as if she were preparing to roll a joint of dagga, and began to repeat it, but her voice sounded hoarse and strange, like a classic crackersaurus', and the words did not come the same as they used to do—

Strummm!

"How doth the little cabbage head
Next score some mescaline,
Sell dirt grass from his candy man
To every sucker seen!

How cheerfully he seems to grin,
How neatly rolls some weed,
And jab/jobs with the best of them
Manteca from the Queen!"

"I'm sure those are not the right words," confessed a pathetic, coked-up Alice, and her eyes filled with tears again as she went on in a state of modest lachrymosity, "I must be in a k-hole after all, and I shall have to turn myself in and go and live in that poky little rehab centre in Kapuskasing, and have next to no marathons to swallow, and oh! ever so many cold turkeys to endure! No, I've made up my mind about it; if I'm in a state of ketamine-induced confusion, I'll just crash here and chill out! It'll be no use my concerned parents putting their heads down that man-hole and saying "Come up again, dear, time to read your Bible with your elder sister!" I shall only look up and say "Who the *uck am I? Tell me that first, and then, if I like being that person, I'll come up: if not, I'll stay down here and live off a steady diet of magic mushrooms and california cornflakes—but, oh dear!" cried Alice defiantly, with a sudden trickle of tears, "I do wish they *would* put their heads down and throw me a new maserati and an ounce of cadillac! I am a devout cafeteria-style-user and to score so very little as I am now is a real drag!"

As she stated this she peered down at her hands, and was surprised to see that she had put on one of the teller's kid gloves while she was talking. "How *can* I have done that?" she wondered. "I must be back on eye-openers again." She got up and staggered to the unmarked wooden crate to search for some additional goods, and discovered that, as nearly as she could guess from her reflection in a broken piece of mirror lying in the gutter, she was now slit-eyed with two bruised eyes, her face covered in lithium scabs, her dried mouth missing at least six teeth, and both her cheeks were shaking rapidly, calligraphed by track marks: she soon found out that the cause of this was the fact that her walk through the sewer served as a cold turkey and a time to chill out a la canona.

"Cold turkey *accompli* and now one hundred percent . dishabituated! That was a narrow escape from a junkie grave!" admitted Alice, a good deal frightened at the sudden change, but very glad to find herself clean again; "and now for that garden and the fabulous poolside bar!" Around the turn, she ran with all speed back to the little door: but, alas! the little door was shut again, and the house key was lying on the wooden crate as before. Alice tried to face her return to sobriety with heroic fortitude, but alas was finding that life sucks when you're clean "and things are frigging worse than ever," concluded the pathetic, ebriated child, sliding into a panic, "for I never was so in need of a fix as this before, never! And I do declare it's too bad, that it is!"

Just as she had uttered these American-style phrases her foot slipped on yet another classic banana skin, and in another moment, splash! she was up to her chin in laudanum. Her first idea was that she had somehow fallen into one of the

Great Lakes, "and in that case I can bum a ride on a freighter, connect up to the CN railway and hop a freight train, like a genuine beatnik," she calculated to herself. (Alice had been to the seaside once in her life on a family trip to England where she had tried to score some amyl nitrite, and had come to the general conclusion, that wherever you go to on the English coast you find a number of surfers in the sea, some insufferable, spotty children wearing Mickey Mouse ears digging in the sand with plastic spades, then a row of bed and breakfasts in front of a street of lodging houses, and behind them a railway station where all the runners, peddlers, and hookers hang out.) Then she remembered reading with pleasure and avidity her papa's copy of Charles Kingsley's eminently readable *Glaucus, Or, the Wonders of the Sea Shore* and so she found it somewhat dispiriting to discover the pool so empty. Where were the shrubberies of pink coralline, the arborets of jointed stone, the grottoes of madrepores and waving tessellations of kelp? However, she soon ascertained that she was in the Pool of Wet Dreams, made from the very tincture of opium which she herself had bought from a crooked, late-Victorian apothecary (known as Uncle Ben) before this story started, to ease her arthritic, widowed grandmother's pain and which she dropped and broke after her latest fix.

"I wish I hadn't bought so frigging much!" reflected Alice,

as she swam about in a manner reminiscent of one of the three Rhine-maidens immortalized in Wagner's ecumenically acclaimed, four-epic opera cycle *Der Ring des Nibelungen*, occasionally sipping the very cool tincture and experiencing as a consequence a most pleasant vacillating equilibrium of her labia. "I shall be punished for it now, I suppose, by being drowned in my grandma's laudanum! That *will* be a fricking insane thing, to be sure! However, everything is insane to-day."

Just then she heard something splashing about in the pool a little way off, and she swam nearer in the manner of a sociable and curious dolphin to make out who or what it was: at first she thought it must be a walrus or hippopotamus, but then she remembered how hopped up she was again, and she soon made out that it was only a fellow junkie (equally stoned) who had slipped in like herself.

"Would it be of any use, now," ruminated Alice, "to speak to this bedbug? Everything is so out-of-the-way down here, that I should think it very unlikely he can still talk: at any rate, there's no harm in trying." So she began: "Yo junkie bro, do you know the way out of this fu**ing pool? I am very tired of swimming about here, getting baked on laudanum, just like Coleridge. Oh

yo, junkie bro!" Alice thought this must be the proper manner of addressing a drug-dependent *homo erectus*: she had never done such a thing before (for she was a solitary user), but she remembered having seen her brother do it many times when he sold pony packs of crack to several of them. "A junkie—of a junk—to a junky—a junky—O junkie!" The junkie looked at her rather inquisitively on hearing this curious, egregious, mantra-like emission, and seemed to her to wink with one of his half-closed blood-shot eyes, but he uttered **ck all.

"Perhaps the asshole doesn't understand English," Alice conjectured, wiping some laudanum out of her eyes with her grubby knuckles and transferring it to her lips and tongue; "I daresay he's a French-speaking Québécois junkie from Montréal or Sept-Îsles, come over with Jean Genet or Samuel de Champlain." (For, with her scant knowledge of Canadian history and being so banged, Alice had no very clear notion how long ago anything had happened.) So she began again: "*Où est mon petit junkie?*" which was the first sentence in her Joual Drug Slang Dictionary that was typeset throughout in italics. The junkie gave a sudden leap out of the laudanum as if a participant in some synchronized swimming contest, and seemed to quiver all over with either sheer discomposure and extreme disquietude or else severe withdrawal symptoms. "Oh, I beg your pardon!" added Alice hastily, afraid that she had hurt the poor fellow's feelings. "I quite forgot you didn't like French Canadians."

"Not like French-Canadian cops!" cried the junkie, in a shrill, passionate voice. "Would you like the French Canadians if you were me?"

"Well, perhaps not," said Alice in a soothing tone: "don't be pissed off about it. In fact I wish I could show you our local flat foot, Detective David Bracebridge: I think you'd take a fancy to cops if you could only see him. He's the pride of the entire police department and has received loads of awards and commendations from the Chief Commissioner—and he even let's me call him Dave. He's such a dear sweet thing," Alice went on, half to herself, as she swam lazily about in the opium pool in a distinctly unsynchronized manner, "and at night he sits selling confiscated p-funk and debs out of the back of his Ford Ranger parked down a dark alley behind the public basketball court, licking his fingertips before counting the lettuce he's received from yet another illegal sale—and he is such a pushover to bribe and pay off—and such a capital cop for catching dealers who don't pay him his cut—oh, I beg your pardon!" cried Alice again, for this time the junkie was bristling all over and picking at his lithium scabs, and she felt certain he must be really scared or offended. "We won't talk about him any more if you'd rather not."

"We indeed!" ululated the junkie, who was now trembling down to the end of his spine, aching for another fix. "As if I would talk on such a subject! Our family always hated cops: nasty, low, vulgar things! Don't let me hear the name again!"

"You won't indeed!" assured Alice, in a great hurry to change the subject of conversation. "Are you—are you fond—of—of—Columbian dealers?" The junkie kept on jerkily picking at his lesions and failed to answer; accordingly Alice continued as if permission were granted: "Well, there's four or five of them congregate near our house and some of them bring hookers along. I should like to show you some! One's a dark-skinned, brown-eyed kid called Ramón, fresh in town illegally from Bogotá, you know, with an endearing twitch to his nose and eyes, and oh, such black, curly hair and ever so cool tattoos! He's liked on Facebook by Frank Lucas, the famous American gangster and heroin dealer, and he'll trade you a kilo of his polvo blanco in exchange for a heisted plasma TV from Vision Electronics or Walmart! He'll also tip you to the names and locations of other dealers, real thoroughbreds, and ask you for the cellphone numbers of any cabbage heads you might know of who might need a fix, and all sorts of things—I can't remember half of them—and—oh yes, he's also connected to the Mafia, you know, and he says it's so useful, it's worth a hundred kilos of high-grade bazooka! He says the Mob kills all the cops if they move in on his turf for a covert sting and—oh dear!" cried Alice in a sorrowful tone, "I'm afraid I've offended him again!" For the pathetic and enigmatic bedbug was swimming away from her as hard as he could go across the pool of laudanum (with the occasional sip of it), and making quite a commotion as he went.

So she interpellated softly after him, "Junkie dearest! Stop swimming as if you're racing Michael Phelps and do come back again, and we won't talk about cops or the Mob either, if you really don't want to!" When the junkie heard this, he turned round and swam slowly back to her: his face was quite pale (he's feenin badly and desperately in need of a fix, Alice speculated), and he muttered in a low, trembling voice, "Let us get to the shore, and then I'll tell you my history, and you'll understand why it is I hate cops, and French Canadians ones especially."

It was high time to split, for the pool was getting quite crowded with other addicts who had discovered it was composed entirely of laudanum: there was a mule named Damian and a young cokehead executive by the name of Troy, an emaciated hooker called Mavis, a bent Northwest Mounted cop called Ronnie, and a de-frocked RC priest, known in the 'hood as Father Patrick, as well as several other curious derelicts and fellow mortals. Alice led the way, and the whole gang swam collectively to the shore in a manner most antonymic to the Normandy landings on Juno Beach.

CHAPTER III.

A Lamborghini and a Long Tail

They were indeed a fucked-up-looking bunch that assembled on the bank—Mavis the hooker with laddered pantyhose and tight, purple latex loin-tube, badly crumpled and stained with the odd pecker track, the dealers all with shaved heads and tattooed necks, wearing standard baggy pants and Adidas-brand Raptors zip-jackets, their hoods ceremoniously and ritually pulled over their heads in the manner of those seventeenth-century Spanish monks that Luis de Morales immortalized so powerfully on his canvases in predominantly brown and black paint, and all soaking wet, stoned, and looking most uncomfortable.

The primary and most urgent matter of course was how to score again: there seemed to be a severe drought in that part of the 'hood, from acid through zoom, due to several successful drug enforcement busts by the uncle. Accordingly, they had a consultation about this dire state of affairs, and after a few minutes it seemed quite natural to Alice to find herself talking familiarly with them, as if she had known them all her life. Indeed, she had quite a protracted argument with the bad cop, who at last turned sulky, and would only say, "I am older than you, and so I must know better"; and this Alice would not allow without knowing how old he was, and, as the cop positively refused to tell her his age, there was pshit all more to be discussed.

At last the mule, who seemed to be a person of authority among them, called out, "Yo relax and listen up! I know a quick way to end this drought!" They all sat down at once, in a large ring, with the junkie in the middle. "I'll check in with the bomb squad on the adjacent turf and try to score some more of that bolivian marching powder for a starter," he announced. Alice kept her eyes anxiously fixed on him, for she felt sure she would go into bad withdrawal at any moment if she didn't get an armful of the old garbage soon.

"Ahem!" coughed the mule with an important air, "are you all ready? This is the quickest way to score I know. Okay, cut the crap and listen! Cardinal Cruz (covertly a devout member of the Church of Jesus Christ of Latter-day Saints and a co-parishioner with Mitt Romney) is the main supplier to the Pope who knows a balloon merchant in England named Eddie, who has a twin named Roy who runs an amphetamine factory in the south of France who exports a lot to Eastern Europe and South Korea via a chain of dolla boys in Afghanistan, Iran and Pakistan, where it's then shipped by cargo container via Montréal to Boston, where a dealer named Sammy on Boylston Street sells it for $20 a pop."

"Ugh, what the fu*k!" expleted Mavis, with both an asterisk and a shiver.

"I beg your pardon!" responded Damian the dealer, frowning, but very politely: "Did you speak?"

"No fricking way!" garbled the hooker hastily.

"I thought you did," confessed Damian. "—I proceed. The dealer on Boylston's also connected to a fence and ex-badge bunny in Vancouver named Shirley who knows an author in Harlem, known as Dr. Deviant, who'll write her a prescription for anything from ocean city to dead on arrival, plus loads of debs and eccy. This author in Harlem is friends with some beat artists working for a Mob guy in Manhattan named Tony Falsetto, who has the mayor, Michael Bloomberg, on his payroll, who can—"

"Can freaking *what?*" interrupted the currently coked-up and impatient, young executive named Troy.

"Can freaking move *it*," Damian replied rather crossly: "of course you know what 'move it' means."

"I know what 'it' means well enough, when I ask a john to put one on his tongue before I let him move downtown and start carpet munching," interjected Mavis impolitely: "it's generally a cheap, used, latex-rubber one, pink or black, and made in China. The question is, what *can* the frigging Mayor of Manhattan move?"

Damian failed to notice this interrogation, but hurriedly went on, "—move the shipment from the f***ing factory in France back to Cardinal Cruz, who you remember is the main supplier to the Vatican, who then gets it by private papal Learjet to a different fence in Columbia named Francesco who gets it to—how are you getting on now, my dear?" he continued, turning to Alice as he outlined the logistical network of delivery.

"As frigging needy as ever," answered Alice in a curt yet honest tone: "it doesn't seem a quick way to score to me at all." (It did indeed seem as if simplicity had become the final refuge for complexity.)

"In that case," continued Damian with ersatz solemnity, rising to his feet, "I move that the meeting be adjourned, for the immediate adoption of more energetic remedies to secure abolics, devil dust, wacky weed, schmeck—"

"Speak Canadian-English!" demanded Ronnie, the bad barney. "I don't know the location of half those fuc**ng places, and, what's more, I don't believe you do either!" And as the dealer bent down his head to obfuscate a grimace of laughter, some of the other bedbugs threw up chunks audibly.

"What I was going to say," Damian continued in a highly sarcastic tone, "was, that the best pshit to get us high again would be a lamborghini full of liquid lady."

"What the hell *is* a lamborghini?" inquired Alice, adducing authentic irritation; not that she wanted much to know, but the dear little dealer Damian had paused as if he thought that somebody ought to speak, and no one else seemed inclined to say anything.

"Why," informed Damian, "it's like a maserati and the best way to explain it is to make one." (And, as you little readers might like to try this thing yourself, some hot summer evening or some cold winter day, I will tell you how the dealer managed it.)

First he downed the contents of a half full mickey of Captain Morgan rum, then he washed out the bottle and took off the rubber cover of a spark plug from an abandoned Dodge Ram conveniently deposited by the congeries, which he put over the mouth of the bottle, that way producing an ingenious crack pipe ("the exact brand of rum doesn't matter," Damian moved to reassure). Next he filled it with the best of his high-quality real tops, after which all the party were gathered in a circle next to each other (at least the ones who could still stand). There was no "One, two, three, and away," but they began smoking when the lamborghini was passed to them, and each left off at their pleasure. However, when they had been smoking half an hour or so, and were quite razed again, Damian suddenly called out "The joypop's over!" and they all crowded round him, panting, and asking, "But where the fornication's the rest of the ready rock?"

This question the dealer couldn't answer without a great deal of excogitation (for he too was quite razed), and he sat for a long time dribbling with one finger pressed upon his forehead (the position in which you usually see Shakespeare in the pictures of him painted prior to 1697, or that nude, eponymous thinker in the corny 1902 sculpture by the noted but hugely overrated French artist Auguste Rodin), while the rest waited in silence. At last Damian managed to reiterate with persuasive lucidity, "*The joypop's over and we need to score some more.*"

"But which specific bedbug is to get the new addition?" quite a chorus of junkie voices inquired.

"Why, *she*, of course," uttered Damian victoriously, pointing to Alice with one extremely trembling index finger; and the whole party at once crowded round her, calling out in a confused way, "New addition! New addition!"

Faced with this demand Alice found herself lost for any idea of what to do, and in despair thrust her hand in her huge purse, the kind carried by sex workers, and pulled out a crumpled pony pack of new jack swing (luckily the laudanum had not got into it), and handed it round. There was exactly one a-piece all round.

"But she must have some herself, you know," insisted the surprisingly courteous and unselfish crack hoe.

"Of course, Mavis," Damian replied very gravely. "What else have you got in your hooker-style purse, Miss Alice?" he went on, turning to the same little girl.

"Only a nickel bag of pac man," confessed Alice sadly.

"Hand it over here," requested the dealer.

Then they all crowded round her once more, while Damian solemnly presented the bag of pac man, saying "We beg your acceptance of this excellent grade of ecstasy;" and, when he had finished this short speech, they all cheered before barfing.

Alice thought the whole thing was quite absurd, but they all looked so amped and potentially violent that she was too scared to laugh; and, as she could think of nothing at all to say, she simply bowed, and took the swedge, looking as solemnly grateful as she could.

The next thing was for Alice to ingest the mooker: this caused some noise and confusion, as the other bedbugs complained that after backing and back-jacking they all shot up a bad bundle. The hooker, Mavis, choked badly and had to be violently patted on the back. However, it was over at last, and they sat down again in a circle, Bedouin-style, and begged Damian to deal them something more.

"You promised to sell me a nick of nexus, you know," Alice reminded Damian, "and why the intercourse is it you don't have any regular c & m," she added in a trembling state of withdrawal, half afraid that he would be offended once more.

"Mine is a long and a sad tale!" commenced the junkie from the pool, turning to Alice and sighing.

"Just get the copulation on with it, I need a fix," responded

Alice vituperatively, staring with desperation at Damian's replete feedbag; "but why do you call it sad?" And she kept on puzzling about it while the junkhead was speaking, so that her idea of his sad tale was something like this—

Strummm!

"Acidhead
said to a
tester, that he
met in the
c joint,
'Let us
both go do
serial speed-
balling: I will
obtain it for
YOU. —Come,
I'll take no
denial: We
must have a
fix; For
really this
morning I've
had fu*k all
but the
agonies.'
Said the
acidhead to the
tester, 'Such
a drag,
dear man,
With
no aeon flux

                    or kaksonjae,
                  we'll be
              strung
          out with
              feenin.'
            'I'll be
            pusher, I'll
                be buyer,'
                      said the
                  cunning
                    old tester:
                  'I'll
                try the
                  whole
                    batch,
                        and
                  condemn
                  you
                  to
                  baby-
                    sit.'"

"You are not attending!" alleged the junkie, interrupting his sublime philippic and turning to Alice severely. "What are you tripping off to?"

"Sorry man," answered Alice not very pleadingly: "you had got to the fifth bender, I think?"

"I intercoursing well had *not* !" cried the junkie, sharply and very pissed off.

"A knot!" exploded Alice with marked effervescence, always ready to exploit a pun and also eager to make herself useful, and looking anxiously about her. "Oh, do let me help to undo it!"

"I'll do no such thing," emitted the sleepwaker, getting

up and perambulating away from the conversation after the complete and utter failure of the homophonic wordplay. "You diss me by talking such frigging nonsense!"

"I didn't mean to diss you!" confessed poor Alice. "But you're so easily offended you know!"

The junkie only growled in reply.

"Please come back and finish your story about the tester and the acidhead!" Alice called after him. And the others all joined in chorus, "Yes, please do!" but the junkie only shook his head impatiently, yelled "Screw you!" and walked away with increasing alacrity.

"It sucks that he wouldn't stay!" sighed Troy, the crackoholic young executive, as soon as he was quite out of sight; and the old dinosaur Ronnie took the opportunity of saying to his number-one squeeze who only had a baby habit "Ah, my dear! Let this be a lesson to you never to shoot up with bad tar!" "Eat pshitte, Grandpa!" countered the young holster-humper, a tad snappishly. "You're enough to try the patience of a fuc**ng thirst monster!"

"I wish I had my old author here, I know I do!" muttered Alice deliriously, addressing nobody in particular. "He'd facilitate some pharming and would soon script us some thai sticks to alleviate the current drought!"

"And who's your author, if I might venture to ask the question?" ventured a curious Mavis.

Alice replied eagerly, for she was always ready to talk about her author: "My author's a general practitioner in Moose Jaw, Saskatchewan, ex-KGB I believe, name of Boris. And he's such a capital one for writing scripts! And oh, I wish you could see him when he's high on fantasy! Why, he'll write you another pad of scripts for loads of lady caine as soon as you can pick up your tooter to snort it!"

This speech caused a remarkable sensation among the bedbugs. Some of the users hurried off at once: one stoned old bag bride, way high on blotters, began wrapping herself up very carefully in silver foil, hallucinating that she was a leftover g-rock while remarking "I really must be splitting; the night-air plays pshit with my throat!" and a pusher named Mississauga Mike called out in a commanding voice to his clients, "Come away, yo! It's high time you were all spaced out!" On various pretexts they all dispersed in admirable disorder, and Alice was soon left alone.

"Pshit, I wish I hadn't mentioned my old author in Moose Jaw!" she soliloquized in a melancholy tone. "Nobody seems to like him down here, and I'm sure he's the best author in the world! Oh, Mr. Author! I wonder if I shall ever see you any more!" And here poor Alice began to shake again, for she felt great sadness in her solitude and was feenin badly and just about totally back in the agonies. In a little while, however, she again heard a little pattering of footsteps in the distance, and she looked up eagerly, half hoping that the junkie had changed his mind, and was coming back to finish his story, and Damian too, to supply his famous demo of dimes.

CHAPTER IV.

The Bag Bride and the Pit Bull

It was indeed Samantha, the young bank teller with the shocking-pink hair, now known to be a notorious crack ass-peddler and tricking for a pimp named Jimmy the Switch, trotting slowly back again, and looking anxiously about as she went, as if she had lost something more valuable than her virginity; and Alice heard her muttering to herself, "F**k! My african woodbine! My lace! Oh my late night! Oh my cactus and c-dust! I'll get fu***ng nailed for this, as sure as nebbies are nemmies! Where the f*ck *can* I have dropped them, I wonder?" Alice surmised in an instant that she was searching for her boosted stash, and she, having a highly degenerate nature and desperately needing to score, began pianoing about for them, but they were nowhere to be seen—everything seemed to have changed since her swim in the pool of laudanum, and the underworld, with the abandoned Dodge Ram, wooden crate and the little door, had vanished completely.

Very soon the skanky poon-renter noticed Alice, having returned to a condition of total ebriety, was doing the base crazies and desperately picking the pavement, and called out to her in an angry ambience, "Why, Mary Ann, what the f*ck *are* you doing down there? Take off this moment, and boost me an ounce of acapulco gold and a dram of vodka acid! And make it quick!" And Alice was so pshit frightened of angry crack whores that she ran off at once in the direction Samantha pointed to, without trying to explain the mistake she had made.

"She took me for her co-hoe," Alice said to herself as she ran. "How surprised she'll be when she finds out who I really am! But I'd better take her that ounce of acapulco gold and her dram of vodka acid—that is, if I can find a supplier." As she said this, she came upon a sleazy abandominium confected with graffiti on the door calligraphed in the finest style of Dondi and Revok, and a torn sign with the name "Y. TELLER" written upon it. Missing the pun entirely, Alice went in without knocking, and hurried upstairs, in mounting trepidation lest she should meet the real Mary Ann smoking a real mary jane, and be turned out of the place before she had heisted the acapulco gold and the dram of vodka acid for Samantha.

"How screwed-up it seems," Alice soliloquized, "to be boosting drugs for a hoe fag hag! I suppose my old author in Moose Jaw will be sending me on messages next!" And she began fantasizing the sort of thing that would happen: "Yo! Alice! Get the f**k over here directly, and get ready to get your Uncle Boris a pony pack of marshmallow reds for Jake and Patsy!" "Coming in a minute, Uncle Boris! But I've got to see that the supplier doesn't run out. Only I don't think," Alice reasoned on to the best of her ability, "that they'd let an author keep writing scripts if he began ordering his clients about like that!"

By this time she had found her way into a messy room with torn wallpaper, used condoms scattered everywhere, a packet of marching dust with several zigzag men and with them (as she had hoped) an ounce of acapulco gold and two or three drams of vodka acid: she took up the a-gold and measured out the requisite amount of vee ay, and was just going to down the rest then leave the room, when her junkie eyes fell upon a little bottle that stood near the marching dust. There was no label this time with the words "DRINK ME," but nevertheless she uncorked it and put it to her lips. "I know *something* awesome is sure to happen," she affirmed to herself with unmitigating reassurance, "whenever I eat or drink anything; so I'll just see what this bottle does. I do hope it'll get me stoned again, for really I'm quite tired of being a la canona!"

It did so indeed, and much sooner than she had anticipated: before she had consumed half the bottle, the potent magic took effect and she found her head circumnavigating the ceiling, and off she went on a number-one psychedelic soul-flight. The hallucinogenic substance quickly affected her brain by mimicking serotonin. She felt she was tripping out with Timothy Leary at a Vietnam War protest in Tahrir Square, but suddenly Adolph Hitler appeared in pink chiffon leotards waving a Nigerian gonfalon. She hastily put down the bottle, saying to herself "Holy crap! that's quite enough—I hope I shan't need any more—As it is, I can't get out of this chicken

pshyt hallucination and I now seem to be fellating the Führer—I do wish I hadn't drunk quite so much!"

Alas! it was too late to wish that! No way. She was now once again a total acidhead wigging to the max, and very soon had to kneel down on the floor to keep her balance: in another minute there was not even room for this, and she tried for amelioration the horizontal posture of lying down with one elbow against the floor, and the other arm curled round her head, looking very similar to the engraved portrait of Lord Herbert of Cherbury effected so ably by George Vertue, the noted eighteenth-century English engraver and antiquary. Still she went on wigging, and, as a last resource, protruded one arm out of the window, and one foot up the chimney to stabilize her head and torso, and said to herself the following in a highly stoned voice that sounded as if it were coming from the lips of a death-row inmate in the Prison House of Language: "Pshitte, I'm utterly wasted, now I can do fu** all, whatever happens. What dire deeds *will* befall me?"

Luckily for Alice, the little magic bottle had now completed the entire gamut of its effects, and she began to sober up and was sliding into a yen sleep: still it was a drag, and, as there seemed to be no chance of her ever getting out of the room again, no wonder she felt bummed out.

"It was much more groovy when I was on the wagon," lamented poor Alice retrospectively, "when I wasn't susceptible to the first fix offered me. I almost wish I hadn't gone down that man-hole—and yet—and yet—it's kinda weird, you know, this sorta junkie life! I do wonder what on earth *can* have happened to me! When I used to read about acid trips as a young child, I fancied that kind of pshit never happened in actuality, and now here I am in the process of coming out of one! There ought to be a book written about me and Adolf Hitler, that there ought! And, what the pshitt, when I grow up, I'll write it—but I'm sketching real quick now," she added in a sorrowful tone; "at least there's pshit all acid left to tempt me to resuscitate my weird tripping *here*."

"But then," reflected Alice, "shall I never get any more tripped out than I just was? That'll be a comfort, one way— never to be an old junkie—but then—always to have turfs to check! That would be one helluva drag."

"Oh, you freaked out wigging Alice!" she remonstrated with herself. "How can you learn sober moral conduct here in this drug-infested underworld? Why, there's hardly room for you, and no room at all for any lesson-books in conventional behaviour, such as Richard Allestree's seventeenth-century blockbuster *The Whole Duty of Woman*!" And so she went on, taking first one side and then the other in her regular schizophrenic way, and making quite a goofy conversation of it altogether; but after a few minutes she recognized a familiar voice outside, and stopped to listen.

"Mary Ann! Mary Ann!" yelled the all-too recognizable voice. "Fetch me my ultimate this moment!" Then came a little pattering of feet on the stairs most familiar to Alice. Indeed, she knew it was Samantha hobbling along as best she could in her cheap stiletto heels, coming in search of her, and she trembled till she shook the house, quite forgetting that she was even now about a thousand times as high as the bank teller, and had no reason to be afraid of her.

Presently the teller-hoe came up to the door, and tried to open it; but, as the door opened inwards, and Alice's elbow was pressed hard against it, that attempt proved decidedly futile. Alice heard her say to herself "What a bitch, I'll go round and get in at the window."

"*No* fricking way!" expleted Alice emphatically, and, after waiting till she fancied she heard the teller-hoe just under the window, she suddenly spread out her hand, and made a snatch in the air. She got hold of nothing, but she heard a little shriek and a fall, and a crash of broken glass, from which she

concluded that it was just possible Samantha had fallen down into a methamphetamine lab, or something of the sort.

Next came an acrimonious voice—Samantha's—"Seamus! Seamus! Where the hell are you?" And then a voice she had never heard before, "Sure then I'm here! On a tweak mission for a deck of baby-t, skank ass!"

"On a tweak mission for a deck of baby-t, indeed!" retorted the lot lizard angrily. "Here! Come and help me out of this pile of pshitte!" (Sounds of more broken glass.)

"Now tell me, Seamus, what's that in the window?"

"Sure, it's a joint!" (Coming from Ireland he pronounced it "jow-eent.")

"A joint, you scum bag! Who ever saw one that f**king size? Why, it fills the whole fu***ng window!"

"Sure, it does so, bigorra, me grand, skanky bag bride: but it's a jow-eent of sassafras for all that."

"Well, it's got no business there, at any rate: go and either smoke it or take it away!"

There was a protracted silence after this, and Alice could

only hear whispers sporadically; such as, "Sure, I don't like this pshit, at all, at all!" "Do as I tell you, you e-tard!" and at last she spread out her hand again, and made another snatch in the air. This time there were two little shrieks, and more sounds of broken glass. "Man, what a pshytt-load of meth labs there must be around here!" surmised Alice. "I wonder what those burnt-out geek monsters will do next. Mistaking my arm for a giant cheroot, really! As for pulling me out of the window, I only wish they *could* ! I'm sure I don't want to stay in this geeked-up crack house any longer!"

She waited for some time without hearing anything more: at last came a screeching of auto tires, the slamming of six car doors, and the sound of a good many voices all talking together: she made out some of the conversation: "Where's the quarter bags of racehorse charlie?—Why, I hadn't to bring but one; Jimmy the Switch has got the other—Bill! fetch it here, asshole!—Here, put it in this corner with the others—No, dick-wad, tie 'em together first—you don't want 'em to come apart yet—Oh! that'll do well enough; don't be so copulating particular—Whatever—Here, Bill! catch hold of this bag of rasta weed—Mind that loose old navy—Pshit, it's blowing away! Heads below!" (a loud crash)—"Now, who the fu** did that?—It was Bill, I fancy—Who's to get that frigging hache back?—No way, not me! You do it!—Screw you, I won't, then!—Bill's to get it back—Here, Bill! the big man says you're to go get back that hache!—Whatever."

"Oh! So Bill's got to go and get the hache back, has he?" conjectured Alice to herself. "Sure, they seem to put everything upon poor Bill! I wouldn't be in Bill's shoes even for a good fix of black tar: this fireplace is narrow, to be sure; but I *think* I can kick a little!"

She stuck her foot as far up the chimney as she could, and waited till she heard something (she could not conjecture in the least what it could be) scratching and scrambling about in the chimney
close above her: then, saying to herself "It sounds like a squirrel, but I bet this is Bill," she gave one sharp kick, and waited to see what would happen next.

The first thing she heard was a general chorus of "There goes Bill!" then Samantha's voice alone—"Catch him, you by the trash can!" then silence, and then another confusion of voices—"Hold up the poor f*cker's head—give him some brandy now—No, not that expensive brand, the other. Don't frigging choke him—How was it, bro? What happened to you? Tell us all about it!"

Finally, a little feeble, squeaking voice emerged, ("That's Bill," thought Alice). "Well, I hardly know—No more juice, thanks; I'm better now—but I'm a deal too f*ck*d up to tell you—all I know is that when I searched for the schmack in that there chimney, something comes at me like a frigging Jack-in-the-box, and up I goes like a fricking sky-rocket from Cape Canaveral!"

"Sounds like the perfect high!" giggled the others.

"We must burn that rival c joint down!" yelled Samantha's voice. And Alice vociferated with equal decibels, "If you do, I'll throw the goddamn works at you!"

There was a preternatural silence instantly, and Alice thought to herself, "I wonder what they'll do next! If they had any sense, they'd take the freaking roof off." After a minute or two, they began moving about again, and Alice heard Samantha say, "A barrowful of MDMAs will do, to begin with." "A barrowful of *what*?" thought Alice, for she was not conversant with all the current abbreviated medical terminology that abounded in Plunderland and didn't realize MDMA is short for methylenedioxymethamphetamine, also known as rainbow skittle, eccy, disco drops and rave energizer, and a word she could not pronounce. But she had not long to doubt, for the next moment a shower of said rainbow skittle came rattling in at the window, and some of it hit her in the face. "I'll put a stop to this," she said to herself after swallowing a handful of the skittles, and shouted out, "You mothers had better not do that again!" which produced another dead silence and an uncomfortable hiatus in the narrative.

Alice noticed with some surprise that the skittles were all turning into little tablets of a different, more potent brand of eccy as they lay on the floor, and a bright idea came into her rapidly decaying cerebellum. "If I eat a couple of these hug drugs," she cogitated, "it's sure to make *some* change in my behaviour; and as it can't possibly make me un-fried, it may help me to become perma-fried, I suppose." So she swallowed one of these disco biscuits, and then another, and was delighted to find that she began to experience euphoria, enhanced mental and emotional clarity, sensations of lightness and floating, and a variety of other pleasant hallucinations. As soon as she was feeling these short-lasting effects sufficient to get through the door, she quickly made her exit from *la maison de cracque*, and found quite an *ensemble* of little users and sellers waiting outside. The poor runner, Bill, was in the middle, being held up caryatid-style by two acid freaks, who were giving him something out of a bottle. They all made a rush at Alice with knives and baseball bats the moment she appeared; but she ran off as hard and fast as she could, and soon found herself safe in a public john.

"That was quite a turf war I landed in," Alice reflected to herself. "The first thing I've got to do," as she sat down on the crapper to catch her breath, "is to get loaded again; and the second thing is to find my way into that grungy abandominium. I think that'll be the best plan."

It sounded an excellently cool course of action, no doubt for a perma-fried junkie, and very neatly and simply arranged; the only difficulty was that she hadn't the slightest idea how to set about it; and while she was picking about anxiously among the used rubbers on the floor hoping to land on some blow, a loud sharp bark just over her head made her look up in a great hurry.

An enormous pit bull, with a studded collar round its neck and no perceivable owner, was looking down at her with large round eyes, and feebly stretching out one paw, trying to touch her. "Poor little mutt!" remarked Alice, in an empathetic tone, and she tried hard to whistle to it; but she was terribly frightened all the time at the thought that it might be rabid, in which case it would be very likely to bite her, in spite of all her coaxing, like the hound of the Baskervilles bit Sherlock Holmes.

Hardly knowing what she was doing, but feeling desperate, she went down on her knees on further carpet patrol through all the stalls and finally picked up triumphantly a small quantity of lady snow, and held it out to the fierce canine; whereupon the dog sniffed it, jumped into the air off all four paws at once, with a yelp of delight, rushed at the casper, and made believe to lick it up; then Alice dodged into an open stall, locked the door and tried to block the open base with her huge

hooker-style purse, to keep herself from being attacked; and the moment she threw out some more powder from her private holdings, the hound made another rush at the easy score, and tumbled head over heels in its hurry to lick and sniff it all up; then Alice, thinking the ferocious fido was very likely to be sufficiently cooked by now and hooked for life, and expecting every moment to be ripped apart by its enormous fangs, made a dash out of the cubicle again; then the mutt began a series of short charges at the young little eastside player, running a very little way forwards each time and a long way back, as if performing a canine barn dance, and barking hoarsely all the while, till at last it passed out a good way off, panting, with its tongue hanging out of its mouth and eventually dangling into an unflushed toilet bowl, with its great eyes half shut.

With the canine interlude abated, this seemed to Alice an excellent opportunity for making her escape; so she set off at once, and ran till she was shagged out and breathless, and the wasted mutt's bark sounded quite faint in the distance. "And yet what a dear little pit bull it was!" remarked Alice in a sensitive afterthought, as she leant against a drunken derelict to rest herself, and fanned her flushed face with one of her extra-large vegas: "I should have liked teaching it how to attack babies in prams very much, if—if I'd only been less lit up to do it! Oh merde! I'd nearly forgotten that I've got to puke again!" (By now Alice was feeling some of the negative consequences of her recent MDMA abuse. Her serotonin activity was seriously demolished resulting in potentially unprovoked aggressive behaviour and severe mood swings.) "Let me see—how is it to be managed? I suppose I ought to eat or drink something or other not very pleasant and with a few spoonfuls of salt in it; but the great question is, what?"

After this providential escape from her latrinal adventure the great question certainly was, what? Alice rummaged all through her vast purse for the indian hemp and lakbay diva, but saw nothing that resembled the appropriate substance to shoot, smoke, or snort under the circumstances. Miraculously, however (and Plunderland is a land of miracles, you know), there was a large mushroom growing near her, about the same height as herself; and when she had looked under it, and on both sides of it, and behind it (as if examining a contemporary sculpture in some metropolitan gallery of art), it occurred to her that she might as well look and see what was on the top of it.

So she stretched herself up on tiptoe, and peeped over the edge of the mushroom, and her eyes immediately met those of a chronic burnout, who was sitting on the top with his arms folded, quietly smoking some good stuff from a long hookah, and taking no notice of her or of anything else.

CHAPTER V.

Advice from a Chronic Burnout

The chronic burnout and Alice looked at each other for some time in silence; he wore a coarse, unkempt celadon pelisse over a badly worn, clerical-grey dolman jacket with the waist an inch or two below his armpits and would have looked most appropriate sitting cross-legged on a beanbag giving the peace sign. His visage bore a strong resemblance to a relief map of the Adirondacks with a smile approximating the *Dies Irae*: at last the Chronic extracted the hookah out of his mouth (with great reluctance I might add), and addressed her in a languid, sleepy voice.

"What's your disease, baby girl?"

This was not a highly encouraging opening for a conversation (and barely audible). Alice replied, rather eagerly, "I'm a general cafeteria-style-user and a bit of a cabbage head when I need to be. I was clean when I got up this morning, but I think I must have been a-boot several times since then."

"What do you mean by that?" dribbled the Chronic, slowly inhaling seconds and thirds of the fallbrook redhair. "Explain yourself!"

"I can't explain *myself*, I'm afraid, dickhead," scoffed Alice, "because I'm not myself, you see."

"I don't see," returned the tea-head, "is this an existential or an ontological problem?"

"I'm afraid I can't put it more clearly," Alice replied with the acme of politesse politely, anxiously waiting to be offered a complimentary toke, "for I can't understand it myself to begin with; and being on so many highs from so many different narcotics in a day is so confusing."

"No, it isn't," insisted the Chronic.

"Well, perhaps you haven't found it so yet," replied Alice; "but when you have to beg for a demo of fast white lady, or piano on the floor—you will some day, you know—and then after that you have to check yourself into a drug rehab centre, or worse, you find yourself languishing in Penetanguishene, I should think a lifetime sampler like you would feel it a little weird."

"Not one bit," countered the Chronic, scratching the back of his head with his big toe.

"Well, perhaps your withdrawal symptoms may be different, or perhaps you're a Buddhist, or stuff like that, they've got ever so much self-control those, Buddhist monks and a pshit load of willpower," informed Alice eagerly; "all I know is it would feel totally weird to *me*."

"You!" said the wastoid dreamily. "What's your poison, baby girl?"

Which brought them back again to the beginning of the conversation. Alice felt somewhat pissed off by the perma-fried's habit of emitting very short remarks, and she drew herself up and said with carefully calculated gravity, "I think you ought to tell me what's you're disease, first."

"Why?" drawled the dinosaur almost inaudibly.

Here was another puzzling question; and as Alice could not think of any good reason, and as the Chronic seemed to be in a *very* unpleasant state of mind, she turned away.

"Come back!" he called after her. "I've something important to say!"

This sounded promising, certainly: obediently, Alice turned and came back again.

"Stay wasted," advised the devout doper.

"Is that all?" queried Alice, swallowing down her anger as well as some XTC in the best manner that she could.

"No way," verbalized the Chronic.

Alice thought she might as well wait, as she had nothing else to do, and perhaps after all he might tell her something worthy of her patient audition. For some minutes he puffed away without speaking, but at last he unfolded his emaciated, scabby arms, took the hubbly bubbly pipe out of his mouth again, and declared, "So you think you're fried, do you?"

"I'm totally sure of it," affirmed Alice; "my serotonin production's all fucked up and I can't remember things as I used to—and I don't keep on the wagon for ten minutes together!"

"Can't remember *what* things?" countered the highly stoned weed meister.

"Well, I've tried to say '*How Doth the Little Lady Caine,*' but it all came out different!" Alice informed in a touchingly melancholy voice.

"Repeat, '*You are Stoned, Father William,*'" commanded the Chronic.

Alice knocked back another disco biscuit, folded her hands, and complied with his behest—

Strummm!

"You are stoned, Father William," the young man said,
"And your speech is beginning to slur;
And yet you incessantly shoot up again—
Do you think it is wise to, dear Sir?"

"In my youth," Father William replied to the man,
"I feared it might injure the brain;
But, now that I'm sure that I do not have one,
Why, I do it again and again."

"You are baked," said the youth, "as I mentioned before,
And have grown most uncommonly thin;
A junkie condition, I've seen it before—
With lithium scabs on your chin!"

"In my youth," said the hype, as he shook his grey locks,
  "I kept myself high with a viper
And the use of this angie—one dollar the box—
  I bought from a renegade sniper."

"You are wired," said the man, "and your jaws are too weak
  For nothing more tough than a vega;
Yet you finished the smack, back to back with the tweak—
  That's the junkie's alpha and omega!"

"In my youth," said the tea-head, "I took to the street,
  And bought crack to back jack from a dealer;
And the positive high it gave me? oh my
  Has made me the last real free-wheeler."

"You are amped," said the youth, "one would hardly suppose
  That your eye was as steady as ever;
Yet you balanced a roach on the end of your nose—
  What made you so awfully clever?"

"I have answered three questions, and that is enough,"
  Said the tweaker; "just listen to me!
Do you think I can listen all day to such stuff?
  **ck off, now, and score me some c!"

"That's all wrong, baby girl," judged the Chronic in the severe manner of a Simon Cowell.

"Not *quite* right, I'm afraid," admitted Alice, hazily; "some of the words have got altered coz I too am loaded—just like Father William."

"It's wrong from beginning to end," he attested with

absolute conviction, and there was silence for some minutes during which time he lit up again.

The Chronic was the first to break this taciturnity.

"What disease would you prefer, baby girl?" he inquired.

"Oh, I'm not particular as to the substance," Alice hastily replied; "just as long as I get krunked up, you know."

"I *don't* know," responded the vintage dinosaur with irritating probity.

Alice said zilch: she had never been so much contradicted in her life before, and she felt that she was losing her temper.

"Are you content now?" queried the cabbage head.

"Well, I should like to be a *little* wasted, if you wouldn't mind," answered Alice: "three hours is such a wretched time to be ebriated and I can feel the munchies coming on pshitte-quick."

"It's a very good high indeed!" insisted the Chronic with

more than a modicum of righteousness, rearing himself upright as he spoke (it was exactly a three-minute high).

"But I'm not used to it!" pleaded poor, shaky Alice in a most piteous tone as she thought to herself, "I wish that chronic asshole would offer me a toke of his shisha pipe!"

"You'll get used to it in time," crooned the Chronic; and he put the hookah into his mouth and began toking again.

This time Alice waited patiently until the Chronic chose to resume their intercourse. In a minute or two he took the hookah out of his mouth and yawned once or twice, then shook himself. Eventually he got down off the mushroom, and ambled away in the grass, merely remarking as he went, "One capsule will give you an upper, and the other will give you a downer."

"One capsule of *what*? The other capsule of *what*?" pondered Alice earnestly to herself.

"Of the shroom dickhead," shouted the now long-distance junkie, just as if she had asked it aloud; and in another moment he was out of sight.

"That giant mushroom must be a psilocybin," Alice concluded, looking more optimistically than thoughtfully at the mushroom for a minute, trying to make out where the two capsules were hidden and finding this a most mind-boggling problem. However, at last she stretched her arms around the stipe as far as they would go, and broke off a bit of the hymenium underneath the pileus with each hand. "Not exactly the capsule I expected, but beggars can't be choosers," she self-averred and nibbled a tad of the right-hand bit to try the effect: the next moment she started to experience a slight nausea that soon passed into distorted sensations of touch, sight, sound and taste, along with increasing nervousness and tangible paranoia.

She was a good deal frightened by this very sudden metamorphosis and felt that there was no time to be lost, as she was now seriously tripping; so she set to work at once to eat some of the alternative portion. Her chin began to feel distorted and seemed connected to her left ear, while her feet seemed to protrude from her mouth in the manner of an early medieval illuminated grotesque, and there was hardly room to open it; but she did it at last, and managed to swallow a morsel of the left-hand bit.

*   *   *   *   *   *

*   *   *   *   *

*   *   *   *   *   *

The piece was easing powder and Alice soon started to feel its effects: drowsiness, pupil constriction, and fatigue. "Hallefu**inglujah, my head's free at last, I've come down successfully!" exclaimed Alice in a tone of sleepy delight, which changed into alarm in another moment, when she found that her capacious purse containing all her rigs and feed was nowhere to be found: all she could see, when she looked down, was an immense array of empty triple-folds, which seemed to float far below her, as plastic islands do in a sea of green leaves.

"What *can* all that green stuff be?" inquired Alice to herself. "I hope I'm still not hallucinating from that shroom. Hopefully it's giggle weed and I can blow a stick or two. And what's happened to my bag? And oh, my poor head, how is it that you're spinning so much?" She was checking out the triple-folds for residue as she spoke to that specific body part, but no result seemed to follow, except a little shaking among the fallen green leaves.

As there seemed to be no chance of her staying around the turn for long, she was content in continuing to check the triple-folds, and was delighted to find that one contained an ample amount of bernie's gold dust. She had just succeeded in inhaling some up her left nostril, and was going to dive in among the folds for more, when a sharp hiss made her draw back in a hurry: a large tout was standing before her, gesturing with one hand.

"Need a fix, doll face?" inquired the tout, "I've a couple of trambos lined up just around this corner. Alternatively I can fix you up with the address of a convenient get-off house."

"I'm *not* sure!" remarked Alice indignantly. "In my own time! I have to check out all these triple-folds first and if that green stuff really is giggle weed then I'll have ample gear for free."

"Need a fix? I say again!" repeated the tout, but in a more subdued tone, and added with a fatalistic sob, "I've tried to find a potential buyer all day, and nobody seems to be needing!"

"I haven't a frigging clue what you're talking about," responded Alice.

"I've tried to turn them on to bermuda triangles, high-quality belushis, viper weed, toss-ups, and tornados, and I've even tried new addition, not to mention goodfellas and jay smokes," the tout mumbled on, without attending to her; "but those fussy buyers! There's no pleasing them!"

Alice was more and more puzzled by the substance of this soliloquy, but she thought there was no use in saying anything more till the tout had quit yakking on.

"As if it wasn't trouble enough packaging the jamaican red hair," grumbled the tout; "but I must be on the look-out for buyers night and day! I'm working harder than a superannuated rent boy. Why, I haven't had a wink of sleep these three weeks!"

"I'm very sorry you've been annoyed, Mr. Tout," responded Alice consolingly, who was by now beginning to dig his problem.

"And just as I'd made what I thought was a sale," continued the tout, raising his voice to a high, falsetto shriek, "and just as I was thinking I should make a sale at last, the son of a bitch walked away!"

"But I'm *not* a buyer right now, I tell you!" affirmed Alice.

"I'm a—I'm a—"

"Well! *What* the fu*k are you?" asked the tout, angrily intercepting her echolalia. "I can see you're somewhat lit up!"

"I—I'm a little girl," confessed Alice, rather doubtfully, as she remembered the number of trips she had gone through that day.

"A likely story indeed!" dismissed the tout in a tone of the deepest contempt. "I've seen a good many little girls in my time, but never *one* with so many track lines on her arms and legs! No, no! You're a heavy user all right and there's no use denying it. I suppose you'll be telling me next that you've never swallowed a lid popper!"

"I *have* swallowed lid poppers, certainly, and in abundance," assured Alice, who was a very truthful junkie; "little girls swallow lid poppers and liberty caps quite as much as male hookers do, you know."

"I don't fricking believe it," remarked the tout; "but if they do, then they're on their way to becoming ineluctably incurable raspberries, that's all I can say."

This was such a new idea to Alice, that she was quite silent for a minute or two, which gave the tout the opportunity of adding, "You're looking for a fix, I know that well enough; and I don't care a rat's ass whether you're a little girl or a hustler."

"It matters a good deal to *me*," countered Alice hastily; "but I'm not looking for a fix, as it happens; and if I was, I shouldn't want to buy from *you*: I don't like gaffles."

"Well, piss off, then!" yelled the tout in a sulky tone, as he settled down again to lurk in a dark corner. Alice adjusted her tight-fitting underwear around her perineum, then crouched down to carpet-patrol among the triple-folds as well as she could, for her lithium scabs kept itching, and every now and then she had to stop and scratch them. After a while she remembered that she still held the remaining morsels of silly putty and gondola in her hands, and so she set to work with the utmost of care, nibbling first at one and then at the other, sometimes tripping high and sometimes gliding on a downer, until she had succeeded in bringing herself down to a nominal state of glazed sedation.

It had been way since when she'd been anything near clean, that it felt quite weird at first; but she got used to it in a few minutes, and began talking to herself, as usual. "Come, there's half my plan done now (whatever it is)! How amazingly puzzling all these highs are! I'm never sure what pshitte I'm going to inject or ingest, from one make up to another! However, I've got myself around the turn relatively speaking: the next thing is, to get into that beautiful *hortus conclusus* with its awesome poolside bar and crash that fabulous party going on inside—but how is that to be done, I wonder?" As she stated this, she came suddenly upon a vacant lot with a derelict get-off house at the end of it about four hundred yards away. "Whatever geeks live there," ruminated Alice, "it'll never do to come upon them *this* clean: why, I should frighten them out of their freaking wits!" So she began nibbling at the right-hand bit again and left the big O alone, and did not venture to go near the house till she had brought herself up a little.

CHAPTER VI.

Maseratis and Monkey Dust

For a minute or two she stood looking at the c joint, and wondering what to do next, when suddenly a dealer in a pair of most picturesque ripped jeans came running across the street— (she considered him to be a dealer because he was wearing ripped jeans: otherwise, judging by his face only, she would have called him "Brad Pitt only taller")—and rapped loudly at the door with his knuckles. It was opened by another dealer likewise accoutred in ripped jeans, with a rotund face and large, protruding eyes reminiscent of Peter Lorre's in the 1941 movie *The Maltese Falcon*, and both dealers, Alice noticed, powdered

their noses with a pinch of teenager as they conversed. By now she too was dying to go on a sleigh ride and also felt very curious to know what their conversation was all about, and crept a little way out of the corner to eavesdrop.

The dealer who had eyes like Peter Lorre's in *The Maltese Falcon* began by producing from under his arm a substantial pouch of dead on arrival, nearly as large as himself, and this he handed over to the other, saying, in a solemn tone, "For the Duchess. An invitation from the Queen to get high." The other dealer, who Alice thought looked like Brad Pitt only taller, repeated with identical solemnity, only changing the order of the words a little, "From the Queen. An invitation for the Duchess to get high."

Then they both high-fived each other, and their fingers got entangled together. Alice laughed so much at this most ludicrous fusion, that she had to run back around the corner for fear of their hearing her; and when she next peeped out, the dealer who looked like Brad Pitt only taller was nowhere to be seen, and the other was sitting on the ground near the door, staring stupidly up into the sky with his Peter Lorre look-alike retinas.

Alice went timidly up to the door, and knocked.

"There's no use in knocking," stated the Lorre look-alike, "and that for two reasons. First, because I'm on the same side of the door as you are; secondly, because they're making such a noise inside, no one could possibly hear you." And certainly there was a most extraordinary pandemonium ensuing within—a constant howling and sneezing, and every now and then a great cacophonous crash, as if a dish or kettle had been broken to pieces and all to the background sound of heavy metal Alice Cooper from a ghetto blaster.

"Please, then," queried Alice, "how am I to get a fix?"

"There might be some sense in your knocking very loudly, and asking for Miguel," the dealer went on without attending to her, "if we had the door between us. For instance, if you were *inside*, you might knock, and I could let you out, you know." He was looking up into the sky all the time he was speaking— incontrovertibly blitzed, and this Alice thought decidedly uncivil for a dealer. "But perhaps he can't help it if he's wasted," she remarked to herself; "his eyes are so *very* nearly at the top of his head and they're the size of table tennis balls. But at any rate he might answer questions.—How the f*ck am I to get in?" she repeated, aloud.

"I shall sit here," the hawker most assuredly remarked, "till tomorrow—"

At this moment the door of the house opened, and a large parcel of dank came soaring out with majestic propulsion, straight in the direction of the dealer's head: it just grazed his nose, and landed on the bonnet of a bashed-up, white, 1979 Chrysler LeBaron Town & Country.

"—or next day, maybe," the flame-broiled dealer continued in the same tone, exactly as if nothing had happened.

"How am I to get a frecking fix of pshit?" pleaded Alice again, with a louder, more desperate modulation.

"Are you to get in at all?" inquired the dealer wistfully. "That's the first question, you know."

It was, no doubt, a palpable verity: only Alice did not like to be told so. "It really is a total drag," she posited to herself. "When I'm desperate for a fix I have to patiently listen to a lesson in scholastic logic. It's enough to drive a little Victorian girl to theft or peddling her ass!"

The dealer seemed to think this a good opportunity for repeating his remark, with variations. "I shall sit here," he said, "on and off, for days and days."

"But what am *I* to do?" pleaded Alice, now well and truly exhibiting the DTs.

"Anything you like," answered the dealer, and commenced whistling.

"Oh, there's no use in talking to that son of a bitch," Alice admitted with manifest exasperation: "he's perfectly dance fevered!" And she opened the door and went in.

The door led directly into a large and commodious methamphetamine laboratory, which was full of smoke from one end to the other: the Duchess was sitting in muffled grandeur on a three-legged stool in the middle. An erstwhile voluptuous woman and veritable bodice-ripper, she appeared arrayed in an undulant dress of silver tissue and tulle, spangled with glass bugle-beads, huge turquoise earrings weighing down her earlobes and a salmon-pink velvet flower was pinned perilously at her left shoulder, and, as a consequence, she looked like Empire in its final decadence. She was nursing a huge sack of baby bhang; the cook, a lanky, emaciated female, was leaning over a vast stove taking on a number while stirring a large cauldron which exhibited both the aroma and appearance of bathtub crank.

"There's certainly ample highs in that frigging liquid!" Alice ruminated to herself with instinctive certitude, as well as she

could for sneezing.

There was way too much gaffel blowing in the air, mixed with the usual lab smells of sweet ether and ammonia. Even the Duchess (a hardened sleigh rider) sneezed occasionally, each time wiping her nostrils with an exquisite rose-pink silk foulard. As for the sack, it was bouncing and slipping alternately without a moment's pause. The only things in the lab that didn't sneeze, were the cook, and a large, limpid junkie who was sitting on the hearth and grinning from ear to ear.

"Please would you tell me," pleaded Alice, somewhat timidly, for she was not quite sure whether it was good manners for her to speak first, "why does that junkie grin like that?"

"He's a Cheshire junkie called Aidan," the ripped Duchess replied between shlooks, "and that's why. Hey, fart face!"

She uttered the last three words with such sudden and contrapuntal vituperation that Alice quite jumped; but she observed in another moment that the maledictory interpellation was addressed to the Peter Lorre look-alike dealer sitting outside, still gazing up into the sky, and not to her, so she took courage, and went on again:

"I didn't know that junkies from Cheshire always grinned; in fact, I didn't know that junkies *could* grin, or at least have anything to grin about."

"They all can," informed the Duchess; "if they score a fix, and most of 'em do and come on with a good case of the ganoobies."

"I know pshit zero geeks who do lady white and come on grinning, that's for sure," Alice responded, feeling quite pleased to have got into a conversation with royalty and hopeful of scoring some complementary rasta ganja.

"You know f**k all, period," yelled the Duchess with waxing truculence; "and that's a fact."

Alice thought the discordant tone of this vile, pugnacious animadversion which outshone the rudeness of her own prior confession was totally uncool, and thought it would be as well to introduce some other topic of conversation. While she was trying to fix on one, the Luddite cook took the cauldron of mind detergent off the stove and at once set to work throwing everything within her reach at the Duchess and Aidan from Cheshire—the gaffus came first; then followed a shower of maseratis, mighty mezzes, various tooters, and copious quantities of Ziploc bags containing high-grade monkey dust. The Duchess took no notice of them whatsoever, remaining oblivious to the aerial bombardment and maintaining her legendary *sangfroid* even when some projectile hit her; and Aidan was grinning so much already, that it was quite impossible to say whether the blows hurt him or not.

"Oh, *please* mind what you're doing with that good quality dope and equipment!" cried Alice, jumping up and down in an agony of sincere panic. "Oh, there goes his precious nose;" as an unusually large quantity of monkey dribble went up it.

"If everybody stuck to their own disease," the Duchess added in a hoarse growl, "the dope would go round a good deal faster than it does."

"Which would *not* be an advantage," calculated Alice, who was a genuine all-star. "Just think of how it would mess up the day and night! You see a junkie normally takes twenty-four minutes to come off a high—"

"Talking of coming *off*," said the Duchess, "chop off her head!"

Alice glanced rather anxiously at the cook, to see if she meant to take the hint seriously; but the cook was truly picked up at that moment in our narrative, happily shlooking a phillies blunt as she busily stirred a full half elbow of motorcycle crack, and seemed not to be listening, so she went on again: "Twenty-four minutes, I *think*; or is it twelve? I—"

"Oh, don't bother *me*," responded the Duchess impatiently; "It's such a bummer coming down!" And with that she began nursing her sack again in an indubitably anthropomorphic manner, singing an odd species of lullaby to it as she did so, and giving it a violent shake at the end of every line in a most sadistic manner—

Strummm!

Speak roughly to your little boy,
And kick him when he sneezes :
He only does it on cocaine,
Because he knows it eases.
CHORUS.
(In which the cook and the junkie joined):
"Smack ! smack ! smack !"

While the Duchess sang the second verse of her serenade, she kept tossing the sack violently up and down, and spilling seriously significant quantities of marching powder to such an extent that Alice, who was by now in genuine agonies to the max once more, immediately switched to base crazies and could hardly hear the words—

Strummm!

I speak severely to my boy,
I beat him when he sneezes ;
Yet he can thoroughly enjoy
His smack when e'er he pleases !
CHORUS.
"Smack ! smack ! smack !"

"Here! you may hold it a bit, if you like!" the Duchess informed Alice, flinging the sack at her as she yakked on. "I must go and prepare to get high with the Queen," and she

hurried out of the room. The cook in high dudgeon (à la Gordon Ramsay) threw an entire pan of sleet after her as she went out, accompanied by a litany of oaths and maledictions, and barely missing her.

Alice caught the sack with some difficulty, as it was a queer-shaped large packet not unlike a shaved and lacquered pot-bellied Vietnamese pig, and it held a veritable cornucopia of substances. Alice dipped into its contents, "This looks like good skunkweed and swedge, not to mention this pakistani black and manhattan silver," assessed Alice with compromised certainty. The poor, pathetic junkie Aidan was grinning and snorting like a steam engine when she caught it, and kept doubling himself up and straightening himself out again between grins in the manner of a North Korean dictator when overseeing vast military parades on his anniversary, so that altogether, for the first minute or two, it was as much as she could do to hold it.

As soon as she had checked out the full range of contents (which also included an abundance of sleigh ride, several fatties to twist up into a sort of knot, baby bhangs, silly putty, tardust, microdots, genuine top-grade A I P, marshmallow reds, and even back-breakers), she carried it out into the open air. "*If I don't find an effective stash for this sack of fine merchandise*," ruminated Alice, "they're sure to finish it off in an hour or two: and wouldn't it be a drag to be without a fix?" She said the last words out loud, and the junkie grinned in reply (he had left off freebasing by this time and was well settled into his Cheshire-style ganoobies). "Don't grin," requested Alice with growing disapprobation; "that's not at all a proper way of expressing yourself, you moron."

The junkie curled his lips upwards into another grin again, and Alice looked very anxiously into his face to see what was the matter with him. There could be no doubt that his smirk did not derive from risibility in any way whatsoever and that he had a *very* crimson nose from way too much b.j., much more

like a snout than a real nose; also his eyes were getting extremely small for a regular, common or garden junkie: altogether Alice didn't like the look of him one iota. "Maybe he's got a bad case of the ghoobies, or perhaps the stupid asshole mistook some shooting the breeze for mad dog. But then again, perhaps he's grimacing with pain," she ruminated, and looked into his eyes again, to see if there were any traces of lachrymosity.

No, there were no tears. "If you're going to turn into an overdose," informed an irritated Alice, "I'll have intercourse all more to do with you. Mind now!" The poor, pathetic junkie grinned again (or winced, it was impossible to say which), and the two of them went on for some while in silence, like an aged, married couple watching television.

Alice was just beginning to cogitate to herself, "Now, what the heck am I to do with this frigging sack when I get it home?" when Aidan grinned again, so widely, that she could not help but look deep down into his mouth in some alarm. Disregarding the ulcerated tongue, severe halitosis and remnants of brown and blackened teeth, she peered down at his tonsils. This time there could be no mistake about it: this was neither more nor less than a prime-grade overdose, and she felt that it would be ridiculously absurd for her to watch him further.

So she set the pot-bellied sack down, and felt quite relieved to hide it behind the ghetto blaster. "If I'd been caught with all this boosted gear," she monologized, "I would have been in serious excrement: but it makes rather a desirable hoard, I think." And she began thinking over other various ways of commandeering the contents, and was just saying to herself, "if only I could swap it for some bad bundles—" when she was a little startled by seeing Aidan sitting in a bashed-up armchair but a few feet away from her.

Predictably, the junkie from Cheshire grinned when he saw Alice. He looked alive, good-natured, she judged: still he had way too many track lines (that made him appear like an aerial view of Grand Central Station), and a great many missing teeth, plus ever so many lithium scabs, so she felt that he ought to be treated with respect.

"Cheshire Junkie," she commenced her converse rather guardedly, as she did not at all know whether Aidan would dig the appellation: however, he only grinned a little wider. "Come, he's pleased so far," Alice concluded, and she went on. "Would you tell me, please, which way I ought to go to score some gaggers?"

"That depends a good deal on where you want to get them," replied Aidan.

"I don't care where, just—" said Alice.

"Then it doesn't matter which way you go," interrupted the

grinning dopehead.

"—so long as I get them from *somewhere*," Alice appended by way of explanation and semantic completion.

"Oh, you're sure to do that," remarked Aidan, "if you only walk long enough to the next smokehouse."

Alice felt that this could not be denied, so she resorted to another trajectory of interrogation. "What sort of geeks live in this part of the 'hood?"

"In *that* direction," Aidan replied, waving his right hand round, "lives an acid freak, known in the 'hood as the March Hare (on account of his speedy exits from drug busts): and in *that* direction," waving the other hand, "lives a crackhead called the Mad Hatter. Visit either you like: they're both permanently fried."

"But I don't want to go among perma-frieds," Alice remarked most informatively. "I want a dealer or something, you know, somewhere I can score."

"Oh, you can't help that," the Cheshire junkie reassured: "we're all nikelonians and po-fiends round here. I'm wasted. You're banging."

"How do you know I'm banging?" questioned Alice.

"You must be," said Aidan, "or you wouldn't have come here."

Alice didn't think that proved a thing: however, she continued her questioning, "So how do you know that you're wasted?"

"To begin with," informed the junkie, "a dog's not mad. You grant that?"

"I suppose so," admitted Alice with some reluctance, "apart from that pit bull who finished off the lady snow I managed to piano in a previous chapter."

"Well, then," the junkie continued, "you see, a dog growls when it's angry, and wags its tail when it's pleased. Now *I* growl when I'm needing, and wag my tail when I'm joy popping.

Therefore I'm stoned."

"*I* call it shooting up, not joy popping," stated Alice, overlooking the transverse logic of Aidan's argument.

"Call it what you fuc**ng well like" was the Cheshire-born sleepwalker's adamant repost. "Do you plan to get high with the Queen to-day?"

"That would be truly cool," assured Alice, "but I haven't been invited yet."

"You'll see me there, partying on the heavy stuff," quipped Aidan, and vanished.

Alice was not much surprised at this, she was getting so used to people floating and disappearing. While she was looking at the place where he had been, he suddenly appeared again, sporting his huge, ornamental smile that caused him to resemble an amateur ventriloquist.

"By-the-bye, what became of the sack?" inquired the speedball artist. "I'd nearly forgotten to ask."

"It turned into a pot-bellied Vietnamese pig," Alice answered nonchalantly, just as if he had come back with super flu.

"I thought it would," grinned Aidan, and vanished again.

Alice waited a little, half expecting to see him reappear again, but this time he was a genuine no-show, and after a minute or two she walked on in the direction in which the crackhead called the Mad Hatter was said to reside. "I've seen toss-ups before," she remarked to herself; "I hope this one will be much more generous with his supply, and perhaps, as drugs seem plentiful in the underworld, he won't be doing the base crazies—at least not like I did in that pissoir with the pit bull." As she reflected on this recent misadventure, she looked up, and there was the Cheshire junkie again, horning some goma while he grinned.

"Did you say pig, or fig?" Aidan inquired.

"I said pig," replied Alice; "and I wish the fu*k you wouldn't keep appearing and vanishing so suddenly: you make me feel like I'm on freaking acido."

"Relax, chill out," advised the occasional cotton shooter; and this time he deliquesced quite slowly, beginning with the end of the toes, and ending with the grin, which remained some time after the rest of him had gone, in the manner of a bad surrealist image.

"Well! I've often seen a junkie without a grin,"thought Alice; "but a grin without a junkie! I must be freaking hallucinating!"

She had not staggered in her mindless pilgrimage much farther before she came in sight of the crackhead's pad: she surmised it must be the correct peddler's pad, because she observed him pharming on the doorstep and beside him was a sign reading "COME IN AND DIP AND DAB." It was so derelict and insalubrious a dive that she didn't like to go nearer till she had nibbled some more of the left-hand liberty cap, and got herself wigging once more as its mind-altering potentialities started to take effect: even then she staggered up towards it with indisputable timidity, saying to herself, "Suppose he should try to push me off with some nixon instead of china white! I almost wish I'd gone to see the acid freak instead!"

CHAPTER VII.

A Mad Tea-Party

There was a table set out under an elm tree in front of the house, and the thirst monster and the tail lighter were busy firing the ack ack gun: a diminutive belushi fiend of seemingly female gender was lying between them, near comatose, and the other two were using her as a cushion, resting their elbows on her, and talking over her head. "It must be *very* uncomfortable for that tiny belushiphile," conjectured Alice; "only, as she's so paralytic, I suppose she doesn't care a fu**."

The table was a large one with ample seating, but the three were all crowded together at one corner of it like a trio of Jehovah's Witnesses strategizing their morning canvass: "No dope! No dope!" they expleted when they noticed Alice approaching. "There's *plenty* of goddamn dope!" replied Alice with sublime indignation, and she sat down in a large, worn-out armchair littered with old glass guns at one end of the table.

"Have some golpe, bitch," the acid freak suggested in a charitable, albeit offensive, manner. "There's some unused sharps over by the john door, so feel free to gravy."

Alice looked all round the table, but there was nothing on it except for some acapulco red. "I don't see any china white or any mister brownstone," she informed with a disappointed disposition.

"There isn't any," reassured the crackersaurus.

"Then it wasn't very civil of you to offer it," responded Alice with acerbic indignation.

"It wasn't very civil of you to sit down without being invited, asshole," countered the irritable, crackophile hatter.

"I didn't know it was *your* frigging table," insisted Alice amply matching his belligerency; "it's laid for way more than three. And besides there's a sign outside that says clearly 'COME IN AND DIP AND DAB.'"

"Your scabs need treating," observed the acidophilic hare. He had been looking at Alice for some time with great curiosity, and this was his debut declaration.

"You should learn not to make personal remarks about a sleepwalker's appearance," Alice counselled with measured severity; "it's very inconsequential."

The freak opened his eyes very wide on hearing this; but all he said was, "Why is an addict like a used condom?"

"Far out, we'll have some cool fun now with these Zen koan-style questions!" responded Alice with refreshed effervescence. "I'm glad they've begun asking riddles—I believe I can guess that," she added aloud.

"Do you mean that you think you can find out the answer to it?" asked el loco haberdasher.

"Exactly so," responded Alice.

"Then you should say what you mean," the crackerjack went on.

"I do," Alice hastily replied; "at least—at least I mean what I say—that's the same thing, you know."

"Nowhere near the same!" countered the crazy coverer of heads. "You might just as well say that 'I snort what I mainline' is the same thing as 'I mainline what I snort!'"

"You might just as well say," added the toss-up, "that 'I channel-swim for a daytime' is the same thing as 'I daytime for a channel-swim!'"

"You might just as well say," appended the belushi fiend, who seemed to be conversing in her sleep, "that 'I'm daytiming when I'm evening' is the same thing as 'I'm evening when I'm daytiming'!"

"It is the same fu*ki*g thing with you," insisted the ticket freak most emphatically, and here the conversation came to an abrupt cessation and the party sat in brooding taciturnity for a minute while Alice meditated over all she could remember about addicts and used condoms, which wasn't much (in the matter of the latter).

The acido leporid was the first to break the silence. "When will we chase the dragon?" he eagerly inquired, rotating towards Alice's direction: he had extracted his sharp from out of his pocket, and was ready to start geezin a bit of dee gee, tapping it every now and then, and holding it up to his half closed / half open eyes.

Alice considered a little, and then stated assertively "It's entirely up to you as I have copulate all goods as yet."

"Two ounces wrong!" yelled the acid freak in muffled syllables of conquest. "I told you speedballing wouldn't suit the works!" he added, looking dyspeptically at the insane adorner of cerebellums.

"It was the *best* available mix," the troop head replied with confected meekness.

"Yes, but someone's been tapping the bags," the black sunshine lover grumbled: "also you shouldn't have put it in those triple-folds with that rusty razor blade."

The haberdashing crackhead took the mixture out of his pocket and looked at it despondently: then he dipped some into his cup of laudanum, and perused it again: but he couldn't think of anything better to say than to reiterate his prior remark, "It was the *best* available mix, you know."

Meanwhile, Alice had discovered what appeared to be a couple of black mollies on the floor and downed them instantly to turn on again. She had been looking over the crackerjack's shoulder with avid curiosity. "What a funny speedball!" she remarked. "It goes down okay but doesn't get you high!"

"Why should it?" muttered the southparker. "Do *your* black mollies give you a buzz?"

"Of course not, dick-wad," Alice replied very brusquely:

"but that's because these aren't black mollies but freaking licorice allsorts. I'm just imagining I'm high."

"Which is just the case with *mine*," uttered the soda man in copasetic consonance.

Alice felt dreadfully puzzled. The snowman's remark seemed to have no sort of meaning in it, and yet it was certainly English. "I don't understand a word you said," she replied, as politely as she could, "are you a Modernist writer based in Paris or something?"

"The belushiphile is comatose again," mumbled the sheet-rocking fiend, and he poured a few used glass guns upon her head.

The diminutive belushi freak (who looked like a dormouse) shook her head impatiently, and said, without opening her eyes, "Of course, of course; just what I was going to remark myself."

"Have you guessed the riddle yet?" the third-month leporid asked, turning to Alice once again.

"No, I give up," Alice admitted: "what's the answer?"

"I haven't the slightest fu**i*g idea," replied the ticket head popping some additional sacrament.

"Me neither," added the crackersauran thirst monster as he backjacked a little more scorpion.

Alice sighed wearily, then stated categorically, "I think you might do something better with the time than wasting it asking stupid f*ck*ng riddles that have no answers. For instance, why don't you juggle me some pshyt before I'm totally a la canona?

"But isn't that what life is?" yawned the tiny belushi head in a rare and precious moment of existentialism.

"If you knew Time as well as I do," said the sacramental sipper, "you wouldn't talk about wasting *it*. It's *him*."

"I don't know what the f**k you mean," admitted Alice.

"Of course you don't!" the lens lover responded, tossing his head contemptuously. "I dare say you've never even done Time!"

"Perhaps not," Alice cautiously replied: "and that's because I know how to stay under the radar and avoid getting nailed by the leo. I also know I have to *beat* time when I conduct the school orchestra and I've also done a lot of leapers *in* my time."

"Ah! that accounts for it," declaimed the loony toonsing hare as if suddenly aware of the complex metaphysics of temporality. "He won't stand beating. Now, if you only kept on good terms with him, he'd score you almost anything you like. For instance, suppose it were nine o'clock in the morning, just the *time* to begin getting loaded: you'd only have to whisper a hint to him that you wanted a few blades of locoweed, and there it would appear in a twinkling! Half-past one, *time* to laugh and scratch!"

("I only wish it was," the late-night lover admitted to himself in a whisper.)

"That would be very, very cool," remarked Alice thoughtfully: "but then—I shouldn't be hungry for it, you know," she added with an air of feigned morality.

"Not at first, perhaps," admitted the acid-tweaking hatter: "but you couldn't last past two."

"I suppose you're right," Alice averred with reluctant resignation.

The red lips lover shook his head mournfully. "Not I!" he muttered. "We quarreled last night over a triple-fold of red bullets—just before *he* joy popped with a local raspberry who was taking a break from prowling the curb along the hoe stroll, you know—" (pointing with his kabuki at the belushiphile) "—it was at the great shooting gallery given by the Queen of Cocaine, and I had to sing—

Strummm!

"Puncture, puncture, little vein!
  Now I need some pshit again !"

You know the song, perhaps?"

"I've heard something like it sung in the less salubrious abandominiums," informed Alice.

"It goes on, you know," the lover of rainbows continued, "in this way—

Strummm!

  "Up above the clouds you fly,
  Like the jet stream when you're high.
   Puncture, puncture—"

Here the belushi head shook herself, and began singing in her sleep "*Puncture, puncture, puncture, puncture—*" and went on so long that they had to pinch her to make her stop.

"Well, I'd hardly finished the first verse," remarked the wacky tic-tacky man, "when the Queen jumped up and bawled out 'That dickhead, he's stolen all the tecata! Off with his head!'"

"What a fu***ng drag!" exclaimed Alice sympathetically, "much worse than tapping the bags."

"And ever since that," Monsieur Acido continued in a mournful tone, "she won't juggle me anything heavy."

After ingesting a little thizz, a potentially intelligent question found birth in the remnants of Alice's cortex. "Is that the reason so many tea-heads are put out here?" she inquired.

"Yes, that's it precisely," answered the microdot consumer with a sigh: "it's always a case of searching for an ace, on top of which there's never time to satisfy even a chicken-pshitt habit."

"Then you keep looking round to score, I suppose?" Alice surmised.

"Exactly so, as the airplanes get used up," replied the month after February long-eared mammal with strong hind legs.

"But what happens when you run into a drought again?" Alice ventured to inquire.

"Suppose we change the subject," the shermster intelligently suggested, yawning and thereby dribbling. "I'm getting tired of this frigging crap. I vote the young lady tells us an addict story. Like the late William S. Burroughs did via his cut-up method of narrative composition."

"I'm afraid I don't know one, cut or uncut," intimated Alice, rather alarmed at the proposal.

"Then the belushi-using raspberry shall!" they both cried. "Wake up, belushi tweak!" And they pinched her on both legs at once.

The belushiphile (we'll call her Ramona from now on

as that's her proper name) slowly opened her eyes. "I wasn't asleep," she confessed in a hoarse, feeble voice: "just yippered up. I heard every word you geeks were saying."

"Tell us an addict story, Ramona!" pleaded the scrape and snorter.

"Yes, please do!" pleaded Alice.

"And be quick about it," added the tab-head, "or you'll be asleep stoned again before it's done."

Strummm!

"Once upon a time there were three little buffers," Ramona began at a leisured pace, "and their names were Stacy, Lacy, and Tracy, and they shot up in an attic in a rooming house—"

"What did they shoot up with, the heavy stuff?" interjected the ever-inquisitive Alice, who always took especial interest in questions of snorting and injecting.

"They joy popped chick," answered Ramona, "after smoking three or four a-bombs."

"No way! They couldn't have done that, you know," Alice eagerly amended; "they'd have been laid out with an overdose."

"So they were," intimated Ramona reassuringly; "*very* laid out."

Alice tried to fancy to herself what such an extraordinary way of living would be like, but it puzzled her too much (for the most part because it was exactly like her own existence), so she reignited her line of inquiry: "But why did they shoot up in an attic in a rooming house?"

"Take some more beemers," the seven-up man suggested to Alice, very amiably.

"I've had sweet eff ay yet, asshole," Alice replied in an offended tone, "so I can't take more."

"You mean you can't take *less*," said the astutely correctional tic-tac king: "it's very easy to take *more* than nothing."

"Nobody asked your frigging opinion," retorted an increasingly captious Alice.

"Who's making personal remarks now?" the blotter freak responded triumphantly.

Alice had no idea what to say to this: so she helped herself to some beemers and part of a beautiful boulder, and then turned to Ramona and repeated her question. "Why did they shoot up in the attic of a rooming house?"

Ramona again took a minute or two to think about it and then, after bogarting another belushi, formulated her succinct reply, "It was a crack-attic."

"There's no such fornicating thing in that part of the 'hood; it's always an entire house!"

Alice was becoming decidedly incensed at the tenor of the conversation and aided by replenished vivacity, brought on no doubt by the beemers, decided to continue her critique with full tenacity, but the hare and the hatter warned "Cool it! Cool it!" and the belushi babe sulkily remarked "If you can't be civil to an old skeeger like me, you'd better finish the f*ck*ng story for yourself."

"No, please go on, Ramona!" Alice speedily responded and very contritely. "I won't interrupt again. I dare say there may be one."

"One, indeed!" emoted Ramona indignantly. However, she consented to go on. "And so these three little crack hoes—Tracy, Stacy, and Lacy—they were learning to inhale, you know—"

"What did they inhale?" interrupted Alice, quite forgetting her promise.

"Texas shoe shine and loads of thrust, and after that they would sometimes chase the dragon," answered Ramona without considering at all this time.

"I want a shot of that pineapple," interrupted the rainbow skittler: "let's all move one place on."

He moved on as he spoke, and Ramona followed him: the smoocher moved into Ramona's place, and Alice rather unwillingly took the place of the smoocher. The delicious candy man was the only one who got any advantage from the change in seating and Alice was a good deal worse off than before, as the sniffer had surreptitiously glass gunned the last of the tiger as he moved on past.

There's no way Alice wanted to piss off Ramona again, so she recommenced with calculated caution: "But I don't understand. Who did they score the mustard from?"

"You can buy white boy and sweet stuff from any reputable paper boy," informed the crackhead haberdasher; "so I should think you could buy nurse as well, stupid!"

"But you said they were in the attic," Alice reminded Ramona, choosing not to engage this last remark.

"Of course they fu*k*ng were," declared Ramona angrily after another private belushi; "—well in."

This answer so confused poor Alice, that she let Ramona yak on for some time without interrupting her and entertaining herself with the remaining remnants of the monkey dribble.

"They were learning to use," Ramona continued, yawning and rubbing her eyes, for she was getting very loaded from the lamb's bread and heading for another yen sleep; "and they used all manner of things—everything that begins with an M—"

"Why with an M?" asked Alice.

"Why not?" rhetorically reposted the crazy concealer of skulls.

Alice was silent.

Ramona had closed her eyes by this time, and was drifting off into her yen sleep; but on being pinched by the acidhead she woke up again with a little shriek, and went on: "—that begins with an M, such as m & m and marijuana and morphine and mad dog and mafu and mescaline and magic mint and marshmallow reds and marathon and manhattan silver and manteca and methamphetamine—you know you say things are 'all-lit-up when you've hit sufficient peace weed'—did you ever see such a thing as a drawing of a shroomie?"

"Really, now you ask me," commented Alice, very much confused by this barrage of fresh non sequiturs, "I don't think—"

"Then you shouldn't frigging well talk," interrupted the gick monster.

This latest demonstration of rudeness was more than Alice could bear: she got up in great disgust and walked off, giving everybody the one-finger and yelling, "Up yours!" Ramona passed out instantly, and neither of the others took the least notice of Alice's departure, though she looked back once or twice, half hoping that they would interpellate her: the last time she saw them, they had polished off the mortal combat

and were trying to put Ramona back out on the street to curb-crawl up and down Raspberry Row for some desperately needed lettuce.

"Screw that! I'll never go there again!" announced Alice to herself as she picked her way through the empty beer cans, the half-eaten discarded remnants of pizza, and used condoms that collectively confected the vacant lot. "It's the stupidest goddamn shoot-up I ever was at in all my life!"

Just as she articulated this, she noticed that one of the abandoned houses had a door wide open leading right into it. "That's amazingly weird!" she commented. "But everything's amazingly weird today. I think I may as well go in at once." And in she went.

Once more, thanks to mantic manouevering and an impersonal, omniscient narrative voice, she found herself in the long, low, dingy alley, which was illuminated by a row of homemade oil lamps hanging from the walls, and in close proximity to the empty wooden crate. "Now, I'll manage better this time," she disclosed to herself, and began by fumbling around for the house key, and unlocking the door that led into the garden. However, she desperately needed a make up and so she went to work nibbling a couple of the blue meanies (she had kept a few pieces in her capacious purse for emergencies) till she was tripping out again: then she stumbled down the mind-altered dark and malodorous passage: and *then*—she found herself at last in the beautiful garden, among the bright green cannabis bushes and within spitting distance of the fabulous poolside bar and awesome adjacent Hayward Goldine AquaTrol Above-Ground Pool Salt Chlorine Generator.

CHAPTER VIII.

The Queen's Crack-House

Imagine this scene, dear readers: A dense clump of cannabis plants near the entrance of the place: all of the plants looked healthy (promising a bounteous harvest of acapulco gold) and were so arranged as to form a colonnade of cooling, crepuscular majesty. However, there were three rustic avant-gardeners at it, busily replanting them. Accoutred in the manner of three Italian fascist *carabinieri* with crumpled three-quarter length black capes over their shabby silver-buttoned tunics, they looked like triplets from the *Risorgimento*. On their heads were tricorne hats with blue and red ostrich plumes. Alice thought both their equipage and their demeanour were geeky to say the least, and she moved nearer to watch them. Then, just as she approached them, she heard one say "Look out now, Indica! Don't go bending those stalks like that!"

"I couldn't help it," confessed Indica, in a morose tone, "Sativa jogged my elbow."

On which Sativa looked up and commented, "That's right, Indica! Always lay the blame on others!"

"*You'd* better not talk!" announced Indica with pronounced indignation. "I heard the Queen say only yesterday you deserved to be beheaded!"

"What for this time?" inquired the one who had spoken first.

"That's none of *your* goddamn business, Ruderalis!" expleted Sativa.

"Yes, it *is* his goddamn business, dickhead!" affirmed Indica, "and I'll tell him—it was for digging up the wrong variety."

Sativa flung down his hash pipe and had just begun a speech commencing "Well, of all the unjust things—" when his eye chanced to fall upon Alice, mindlessly adjusting her breasts in her bra as she stood watching them and he checked himself, suddenly embarrassed by his voyeuristic proclivity: the others looked round also and all of them bowed obsequiously low.

"Would you tell me," Alice requested, with more than a morsel of timidity, "why are you replanting those zombie weeds?" Indica and Sativa said nada, but looked at Ruderalis who began to spill the beans in a low voice, "Why the fact is, you see, Miss, this here ought to have been a *Cannabis indica*, and we planted a *Cannabis sativa* by mistake. There's a qualitative difference in the potency of the respective cannaboids you know, and if the Queen was to find it out, we'd all be well and truly up Pshytte Creek, in fact we should all have our heads cut off, de-capitated you know. So you see, Miss, we're doing our best, afore she comes, to—" At this moment Indica, who had been anxiously looking across the garden, called out "The Queen! The Queen!" and the three avant-gardeners instantly threw themselves flat upon their faces. There was a sound of many footsteps, and Alice looked round, eager to see the Queen.

It was indeed a motley entourage resembling a minor humanitarian crisis. All entered the space in seriatim fashion. First came ten dealers carrying copious quantities of g-rocks; these were all wrapped in small packets of silver foil: next the ten takeoff artists, in full kit parade and positively bursting with heisted goods; they were ornamented all over with diamond rings and heavy golden chains, and wore mink coats with black wolf's fur collars as well as black and white patent leather shoes and all in the manner of South Side Chicago pimps walking two and two as baby raspberries do for protection. After these came the speed freaks; there were ten of them also and the dear little geeks came nosegrinding along on skateboards attempting kickflips, McTwists, and Ollie Norths to varying degrees of completion, all on incalculable highs: they were each ornamented with cocaine spoons on silver-plated chains around their necks, and some carried antique bowie knives which they used under their fingernails as well as on the faces of rival gang members. Next came the rest of the addict acolytes, mostly gays, glueys, gick monsters, toe rags, holster humpers, street hookers, conceptual writers and appropriation artists, de-frocked nuns freshly resurrected and still wearing the literary accessories of the 1890s, neo-Nazis, philatelists, assorted members of a doomsday cult, radicalized recruits of the Apache Independence movement, looters and pillagers, miscellaneous reprobates collectively united by their immunity to all moral codes of decency, and one existentialist. Harvey Robespierre, the Pentecostal child molester from Fort Worth, led in the worn strumpets of both genders, transvestites, aged porn stars, Mystic Meg from Manitoba, gigolos, sports celebrities (especially world-famous cyclists stripped of their medals), and among them all Alice recognized Samantha, the young bank teller cum hoe, whose hair was now a stunning electric green: she was talking in a hurried, nervous manner, suspiciously smiling at everything that was said and went by without noticing Alice. Then followed further social pollutants: ten tecatos, Karl Krypton, whose life was a never-ending crime scene, a real King Kong with a massive china cat habit carrying the King's personal crack pipe on a crimson velvet cushion; then came the royal acid freaks and, last of all in this grand procession, came THE KING AND QUEEN OF COCAINE! (The former was Cardinal Cruz, an elegant old pederast and the Queen's main supplier introduced in an earlier chapter, on special loan from the Vatican; the latter a gay pride drag queen from Vancouver known as Melinda.)

The Queen made her appearance *en grande tenue*, albeit in a slightly *démodé* manner, sufficient to evoke the image of some gargantuan wet nurse: her hair was orchestrated into a

huge peroxide-blonde chignon that could be easily mistaken for some unknown urban animal species; she wore a long, strapless, organza gown of alternating black and heliotrope chevrons studiously sprinkled with fresh petals of yellow iris. Her hands were encased in elbow-high, fawn doe-skin gloves, her feet graced by high-heeled, stiletto shoes of sage-green suede, held daintily to her swollen ankles by three breathtaking rose satin cords. Her chubby cheeks were rouged to a rich impasto, applied to mask her valleys of wrinkles and mutinous carbuncular complexion and formed an admirable contrast to the pampas of stubble called her chin. Her carefully applied lizard-green eye shadow on top of a vanilla pigment base provided the perfect bed for her dazzling hot pink, loose glitter, while her eyes were enhanced by fabulous extended Sephora™ false eyelashes, her left thigh being embraced by a rhinestone-studded garter, while her entire body emanated a pronounced odour of *foin coupé*. She truly was an Armageddon of artifice, The Female Eunuch incarnate, the veritable revenge of Caliban, and it all reminded Alice of Queen Victoria's coronation on 28 June 1838, but she was rather doubtful whether she ought not to lie down prostrate on her face like the three avant-gardeners. She could remember sweet fanny adam of ever having heard of such a rule at a shooting gallery, "and besides, what would be the use of a gallery," she reasoned, "if junkies had all to lie down upon their faces, so that they couldn't shoot up?" So she stood motionless where she was, the perfect replica of the Statue of Liberty on hunger strike—and waited.

When the procession came opposite to Alice, they all stopped and looked at her until the Queen inquired with marked and curious severity, "Who is this f*ck*ng nix?" Her interrogation was directed to a parvenu street-guy by the name of Lenny, who was known in the 'hood as the Knave of Hearts, a wise guy cum cyber illusionist of enviable expertise, and an ex-cafeteria-style user who was desperately trying to kick the habit and was now saddled with only a baby one, who bowed and smiled in reply.

"F****ng idiot!" apostrophized Melinda, tossing her head impatiently and, turning to Alice, went on, "What's your name, hoe?"

"My name is Alice, so please your Majesty," answered Alice with strategic, albeit reluctant, politesse; but she appended *sotto voce* to herself, "Screw them assholes, they're not authentic monarchs, they're just a pair of pathetic cotton shooters with serious monkeys on their backs. I needn't be afraid of them! They're totally binged out."

"How the pschit should I know?" amended Alice, baked

yet surprised at the frank display of her own courage. "It's no fornicating business of yours and I'm no hoe."

The Queen turned crimson with fury, and, after glaring at Alice for a moment like some biblical wild beast, screamed "Off with her head! Off—"

"Bullshit! This isn't the fucking French Revolution!" screamed back Alice in a stentorian emission without censorship and in a most revolutionary manner effectively sufficient as to reduce the boisterous and rebarbative Melinda to a coenobitic silence.

His Majesty laid his hand upon Melinda's tattooed and begloved left arm and announced reassuringly "Consider, my dear: she is only a child binger!"

Highly perturbed and truly pissed off, Melinda turned angrily away from him, and said to Lenny the Knave "Turn them over!"

The Knave did so, very carefully, with a single foot.

"Get the fu*k up!" ejaculated Melinda in a shrill, loud voice, and the gallant trio of avant-gardeners (named by their parents after the names of the respective cannabis plants they were destined to cultivate) instantly jumped up and obsequiously commenced bowing to the King, the Queen, the royal acid freaks, and everybody else in a most sycophantic manner.

"Leave the *uck off that!" screamed Queen Melinda. "You make me fricking giddy." And then, turning to the cannabis plant, she continued, "What the crap have you been growing here, kentucky blue?"

"May it please your Majesty" responded Ruderalis, in a highly compliant, though perceptibly stoned tone, precariously going down on one knee as he spoke, "we were trying—"

"I see!" interjected Her Majesty Melinda, who had meanwhile been examining the jamaican gold. "Off with their heads!" and the procession moved on, three of the dealers remaining behind with strict orders to execute the unfortunate avant-gardeners, *not* with the favoured Royal blunt axe (rumoured to be the very same one that chopped off the head of King Charles I), but with half a dozen ten-cent pistols. Panicking and pshit-scared, Sativa, Indica and Ruderalis peed themselves, then ran to Alice for protection.

"No way are they going to behead you three guys!" announced Alice with philanthropic reassurance, and she quickly secreted them in a large, dark-green Chinese-manufactured fibreglass shed that stood nearby and previously contained an awesome botanical a-bomb factory. The three dealers wandered about for a minute or two, looking for them, and then quietly marched off after the others.

"Are their heads off?" inquired Queen Melinda through a thick haze of jay smoke.

"Their heads are *gone*, if it please your Majesty!" the dealers whispered in collusional ambiguity.

"That's the way it should be!" exploded the Queen. "Okay, would you like to speedball or back to back it or simply laugh and scratch?"

The dealers remained taciturn and focused their gaze on Alice, to whom the question was evidently addressed.

"Yes! Let's speedball!" giggled Alice with blithe ebullience.

"Come on, then!" roared the Queen enthusiastically, and Alice joined the rest of the bedbugs, wondering very much what would happen next.

"It's—it's very high quality! Top line, in fact, just in from Acapulco via Miami, the Bronx, and now here in Tronna," informed a timid voice at her side. She was walking by Samantha, who was peeping anxiously into her face.

"Very high quality," declared Alice: "—where's the bonita?"

"Cool it! Not so loud!" advised Samantha brushing aside her awesome electric-green hair in a low yet hurried tone. She looked anxiously over her shoulder, scratching as she spoke and then raised herself upon tiptoe, as in the poem by Keats, put her mouth close to Alice's left ear and whispered "I'm afraid someone's f*cked up. It's a bad bundle."

"How come?" inquired a highly disappointed Alice.

"Did you say 'How cum!'?" Samantha inquired.

"No, I fricking well didn't," countered a mean-sounding Alice: "I don't think it's at all a time to cum. I said, 'How come?'"

"Someone boosted the Queen's pshitte—" Samantha recommenced. Alice and the trinity of avant-gardeners emancipated a delicate rivulet of laughter that soon evolved into uncontrollable guffawing. Laughter, as many know, has parallel benefits to exercise; it can boost your health, support the immune system, improve blood pressure, enhance stimulation

to important organs (especially the bladder), and even reduce pain. But Samantha was undeterred.

"Cool it, you guys!" she whispered in a frightened tone. "The Queen will hear you! You see, her period came rather late this month and the Queen said—" continued Samantha emitting one of the year's best non sequiturs.

"Get to your crack pipes and maseratis!" shouted the already jagged Melinda in a thunderous voice, and all the bedbugs began running about in all directions, tumbling up against each other; however, they got settled down in a minute or two and the smoking and shooting commenced.

Alice was convinced she had never seen such a magical, curious get-off house in her entire life; all scooby snacks and pancakes were complimentary, the scruples and lazy bitches were half price, most of the darts were unused (some even still wrapped in their plastic packets of ten), and the dead presidents were six folds for the price of two. "I'm digging this! It's happy hour in Plunderland among the tattooed denizens of subculture!" The chief difficulty Alice encountered initially was in managing her preliminary deca-durabolin: she succeeded in getting it into a gaffus and stabbed it (comfortably enough) after a little backtracking, into the remnants of a vein in her left arm without her legs giving way, but at the very moment she had started to dart up with some top-grade galloping horse and was going to give Samantha a shot of gaffle, she looked up with such a puzzled expression that she couldn't help almost pissing her pants with laughter: and when she had located another good sewer and squeezed in the g-shot, and was going to repeat the procedure, it was very provoking to find that the gallo had unrolled itself and was in the act of blowing away: besides all this, there was generally an overdose or pass-out in the way wherever she chanced to stagger and, as the doubled-up avant-gardeners were getting up and staggering off stoned to tend their plants, Alice soon came to the conclusion that it was a piss-difficult happy hour to negotiate indeed.

Karl Krypton and the rest of the King Kongs all shot up at once with new jack swing without waiting for turns, quarrelling all the while and fighting for the supply of baby-t, and in a very short time the Queen was in a furious passion and went stamping about and shouting "Off with his frigging head!" or "Off with her frigging head!" about once a minute.

Alice began to feel very uncool about Melinda's mandates: to be sure, for "frigging head" was a junkie phrase the consequences of which she was all too familiar with and besides, she had not as yet had any major altercations with the ferocious tranny faux monarch, but she knew all too well that it might happen any minute, given the Queen's highly choleric disposition, "and then," thought she, in a predictable moment of self-concern, "what would become of my habit? They're dreadfully fond of administering overdoses here, as well as cold turkeys—not to mention beheadings—the great wonder is, that there's any one left alive!"

She was looking about for an effective way to split the scene and wondering whether she could get away without being noticed when she caught sight of a most curious and seemingly paranormal phenomenon in the air: it puzzled her exceedingly at first, but after carefully observing it for a minute or two she made it out to be a familiar grin, and she consequently chuckled to herself "It's Aidan, the junkie from Cheshire, whose grin detaches itself like a UFO: now I shall have some sucker to roll."

"How are you scoring?" asked Aidan, as soon as he'd fully materialized and had finished munching a modest quantity of jelly.

Alice waited till his eyes stabilized again and then merely nodded. "It's no use rolling him," she surmised, "till he's redeveloped a serious belly habit and passed out once more." So she gifted him a nick of nice and easy and in a few more minutes his entire head collapsed to the side. Then Alice put down her black tar temporarily and began rifling through his wallet, pocketing all the lettuce and credit cards (but leaving his ID in case he woke up not knowing who he was), and feeling very relieved, she now had ample scratch to buy loads of those half-price fixes. Aidan initially seemed to think that he was receiving a rubdown from a Japanese sumo masseur and now, out cold and totally comatose, was unconscious and oblivious to everything.

"Notwithstanding the magnificent freebies and deep discounts, I don't think they cut the pshit at all fairly," Alice commenced to mutter with a rather complaining air after counting the boosted lettuce, "and they all quarrel so dreadfully one can't hear oneself shoot the pshit—and they don't seem to have any rules in particular; at least, if there are rules, nobody attends to them—and you've no idea how fricking confusing it is with all the goods being free or bargain-priced; for instance, there's the complementary blue velvet and mortal combat I've got to go through before jacking-up with 5cc of jerry springer— and pshytte, I should have boosted the Queen's vegas of ganja just now, while they were lying on the table!"

"How do you like Her Majesty?" canvassed the recovering junkie in a low-steroid voice and eventually returning his head to perpendicularity.

"Not one bit," replied Alice: "she's so extremely imperious for a tranny and such a castration complex—" Just then she noticed that Melinda was close behind her, listening: so she concluded her sentence evasively, "—likely to mainline, that it's hardly worth trying to keep up with her she is so totally awesome."

The Queen smiled and moved on, a trotting corpulence.

"Who *are* you talking to my dear?" inquired Cardinal Cruz in a deep Tuscan accent, going up to Alice, and looking at the junkie's jet fuel with great envy.

"It's a friend of mine called Aidan—a junkie from Cheshire,

it's in England you know, where all the cats and the cheese come from," announced Alice informatively: "allow me to introduce him."

"Man, I don't like the look of him at all," declared the King of Cocaine most assuredly: "however, he may snort one of my lines of lady snow if he likes."

"I'd rather not," Aidan responded to the Cardinal's surprise.

"Don't be impertinent, dickhead," asserted the Cardinal with great emphasis, "and don't look at me like that!" He got behind Alice as he spoke.

"A junkie may look at a Cocaine Lord," counselled Alice.

"I've read that on some evangelical website, the Biblical Learning Blog I believe, or was it Alpha & Omega Ministries? I don't remember precisely which."

"Well, he must be removed," asserted the Cardinal very decidedly, and he called the Queen, who was passing at the moment, "Melinda, my dear! I wish you would have this junkie removed from the joint!"

Melinda had only one way of settling all difficulties, great or small. "Off with his head!" she commanded mercilessly, without even looking round.

"I'll fetch the executioner myself," affirmed Cruz gingerly, and hurried off.

Alice thought she might as well go back and see how the smoking and jabbing was progressing, as she heard the Queen's voice in the distance, screaming with passion for more mafu. She had already heard her sentence three of the dealers to be decapitated for having missed their turns, and she didn't like the look of things one bit, as the joint was in such confusion that she never knew whether it was her turn to shoot up or not. So she went independently in search of some magic dust.

The said magic dust was in a large porcelain vase along with other kinds of PCPS, which seemed to Alice an excellent opportunity for felicitously narcotizing on a substantial portion of it: especially since her own magic mint had been heisted by Father Patrick (you remember the de-frocked Irish priest from Killarney), who was now freebasing in the basement john.

By the time she had caught him, got the goods back and subducted them beneath her left armpit, the shooting gallery had terminated and both Melinda and the Cardinal were out of sight: "but it's no big deal," thought Alice, assessing the situation with great assiduity, "as everything's free or a bargain here." So she freely succumbed to the blandishment and tucked a sizeable quantity of mad dog away in her enormous hooker-style purse (slipping some extra into her bra) to use later when she needed to freshen up, and returned for a little more conversation with her grinning junkie amigo.

When she got back to Aidan, she was surprised to find quite a large crowd collected round her: there was a contestation going on between a dealer, Cardinal Cruz, and Melinda, who were all yakking at the same time, while all the rest were excrementally quiet, stoned on fresh supplies of psilocybin and kangaroo, and either wigging or intensely baked.

The moment Alice appeared, she was appealed to by all three to settle the divarication, and they repeated their arguments to her, though, as they were all speaking at the same time, she found it very hard indeed to make out what the pshyt was being said.

The dealer's argument (borrowed from Aristotle and grounded cogently in object-oriented ontology) seemed to be that you couldn't cut a bad bundle with high-quality black tar unless there was a bad bundle to cut in the first place: that he had never had to do such a thing before and he wasn't going to begin at *his* time of life.

The Cardinal's argument (borrowed entirely from Maximilien de Robespierre) was that anyone who had a head could be beheaded and that you weren't to talk f*****g nonsense.

The Queen's argument (borrowed from Stalin) appeared to be that if something wasn't done about it in less than no time she'd have everybody overdosed on ten-cent pistols all round. (It was this last remark that had made the entire party of bedbugs look so anxious and frightened.)

Alice could think of zero else to say but, "The pshitte belongs to the Duchess: you'd better ask *her* about it."

"The old fag hag batted out in Montréal last year and is currently in the Centre de Detention Tanguay, doing time for serving nickel deck to an undercover uncle," Melinda informed the dealer without delay: "bribe the prison guards with the usual cookie and free hockey tickets, then fetch her here." And the dealer went off like a car bomb in Kabul.

The dealer's high-grade diesel began blowing away the moment he was gone, and, by the time he had come back with the Duchess (a heavy macaroni dinosaur and occasional bag bitch of necessity), it had entirely disappeared; as a consequence of which both Cardinal Cruz and the dealer ran wildly up and down looking for it, while the rest of the addicts went back inside to make up.

CHAPTER IX.

Aunt Hazel's Story

"You can't think how sexual intercoursing glad I am to see you again, you dear old toss-up!" confided the Duchess, as she tucked her arm surreptitiously into Alice's purse in search of a quick fix before walking off together.

Alice was most relieved to find her so chilled out and giving off such pleasant vibes, and thought to herself that perhaps it was only the marathons that had made her so disputatious and savage when they met in the methamphetamine lab.

"When *I'm* a Duchess," she fantasized to herself quite solipsistically (though not in a very hopeful tone), "I'll have pshit zilch marathons in my kitchen. Manhattan silver will serve me just as well—Maybe it's always marathon that makes people hot-tempered and contestational" she continued, surmising with the few brain cells she had left and very much pleased at having found out a new kind of rule, "and manteca that makes them sour—and pancakes 'n syrup that makes them bitter—and—and a half load of hamburger helper and such crap—that make addicts sweet-tempered. I only wish junkies knew that: then they wouldn't be so stingy about sharing, you know—"

She had quite forgotten the convulsive Duchess by this time and was a little startled when she heard her voice in undesirably intimate proximity to her right ear. "I've been doing time in the slammer on a bum rap. I got the odd satch smuggled into me on visiting days, but I've now got the agonies and desperately need to score. Perhaps your junkie friend from Cheshire has a spare half-elbow or a demo g-shot of fantasy to

appease my esurience."

"Perhaps he hasn't," remarked Alice in a peremptory tone.

"Tut, tut, junkie child!" quoth the Duchess in response. "Everybody here's got goods of some freeking kind, if only you can find them." And she squeezed herself up closer to Alice's side as she spoke.

Alice greatly disliked keeping so close to her: first, because the Duchess had severe halitosis and was truly toe-up grotesque; and secondly, because she was exactly the right height to rest her chin upon Alice's shoulder and it was an uncomfortably sharp chin modelled in the manner of the one belonging to the bottom of the face of the celebrity talk show host Jay Leno. However, she didn't like to be rude, so she bore the symplegma as well as she could.

"The chicken pshit partying's going on rather better now," Alice commented, by way of keeping up the conversation a little. "Is that so," replied the Duchess: "and the red chicken is where?—Oh, I expect that went some time ago!"

"Somebody said," Alice whispered, "everybody in the Oval Office does crack and that's why the office is oval and not round!"

"Ah, well! It means much the same thing to me," confessed the Duchess, her evening increasingly worsening, as she slid her thin, tapered fingers furtively into Alice's capacious purse desperately searching for some mustard or devil's smoke, adding as the words that completed her sentence, "and where the f*ck can I get a cotton shoot? I'm so feenin to the max!"

"How fond she is of asking for drugs!" Alice mused to herself.

"I dare say you're wondering why I don't try to score at the party," the Duchess intimated after a most repulsive rainbow yawn: "the reason is, that I'm doubtful about the temper of the Queen. Shall I try the experiment?"

"*She* might have a bindle or a demo of something," Alice

cautiously replied, not feeling at all anxious to have the 'experiment' tried.

"A palpable verity," uttered the Duchess: "that tranny is quite a cabbage head when she needs to be."

"That's why she's called the Queen."

"Right, as usual," affirmed the Duchess: "what a clear way you have of putting things! Incidentally, what's a bad seed?"

"It's an hallucinogen, I *think*," answered Alice.

"Of course it is," mumbled the Duchess reassuringly, who seemed ready to agree to everything that Alice said; "there's a large amphetamine lab in Richmond Hill run by a Puerto Rican gang—and it's quite easy to break into on weekends."

"Oh, I know!" exclaimed Alice, who had not attended to this last remark, "it's peyote."

"I quite agree with you," vouched the Duchess, "and what do you advise a junkie who decides to kick the habit? 'Be what you would seem to be'—or if you'd like it put more simply—'Never imagine yourself not to be otherwise than what it might appear to others that what you were or might have been was not otherwise than what you had been would you have appeared to them to be otherwise.'"

"I think I should understand that better," Alice confessed very politely, "if I had it written down: but I can't quite follow it as you say it, being as bombed as I am and as convoluted as it is."

"That's nothing to what I could say if I was wired on some antifreeze," the Duchess attested in a strategically maudlin tone.

"Pray don't trouble yourself to say it any longer than that," begged Alice.

"Oh, don't talk about trouble!" uttered the Duchess. "I have to feed the need, just tell me where I can score an iddy biddy birdie powder."

"Perhaps she should ask Father Patrick over there to help

her out, he can be generous when he's amped and not in the
confessional!" thought Alice after freshening up and dusting
her nostrils with her right forefinger. But she didn't venture to
say it out loud.

"Snorting again?" quizzed the Duchess, seizing the
opportunity for another dip of her narrow gnarly fingers into
Alice's enormous marsupial sack.

"I've a right to snort,' demurred Alice sharply, for she was
beginning herself to feel the need to be a little wired.

"Just about as much right," averred the Duchess, "as pigs
have to fly; and the b—"

But here, to Alice's great surprise, the Duchess's voice
died away, even at the start of her favourite phrase "biddy
birdie powder," and the arm that was linked into hers began
to tremble. Alice looked up and there stood Queen Melinda
in front of them in high dudgeon with her arm prepared for
another channel-swim, frowning like a thunderstorm.

"Any birdie powder you can front me, your Majesty!"
began the Duchess in a low, weak, desperate and purposefully
pleading, junkie voice.

"Now, I give you fair fu*k**g warning," shouted Melinda,
stamping on the ground as she emitted a stentorian yell; "either
you or your head must be off and that in about half no time!
Take your choice!"

The hapless Duchess took her choice and cut the scene in a
moment, feenin to the max with the agonies.

"Let's go on with the mainlining," Melinda suggested to
Alice, who was far too intimidated to say a word, but slowly
followed her back to the freshly reopened shooting gallery.

The other addicts had taken advantage of Melinda's absence
and were popping her pills and taking all the fatties out of her
feed bag in the alley: however, the moment they saw her, they
hurried back to the gallery, the Queen merely remarking that a
moment's delay would cost them their heads.

All the time they were jacking-up Melinda never left off quarrelling with the other bedbugs and shouting "Take away his pshit!" or "Take away her hype!" Those whom she sentenced were grabbed, patted down, frisked and cavity searched by the dealers, who of course had to leave off their own mainlining to realize her behest, so that by the end of half an hour or so there were no shooters left and all the laugh and scratchers, except the King, the Queen and Alice, were in agonies and well on their way to another, unintentional and far from desired, sobriety.

Then Melinda desisted, quite out of breath and inquired of Alice, "Have you seen Aunty Hazel, or Aunty Nora or Aunty Mary yet?"

"No," admitted a somewhat puzzled Alice. "I don't even know who they are. Relatives of yours?"

"No. They're the same thing as antifreeze," gasped the Queen jokingly and giggled to the zenith of self approbation.

"I never saw one or heard one," reposted Alice, either ignoring, or not comprehending, Melinda's rather witty pun.

"Come on, then," beckoned Melinda, "and I shall tell you their history."

As they walked off together, Alice strained to hear the Cardinal say in baritone Tuscan *sotto voce* to the general company, "You can have your doobies, eye-openers and black tar back." "Come, That's a good thing!" she said to herself, for she had felt quite dolorous at the amount of confiscated nanoo Queen Melinda had ordered.

They very soon came upon a baked nickelonian who had clearly shot the curb several years ago, lying passed out in the sun. (If you don't know what a nickelonian is, dear little reader, you can look it up in any online Drug Slang Dictionary). "Up, you stoned creep!" demanded the fearsome and insensitive drag queen kicking him several times in the kerbangers with consummate ease, "and take this young lady to see the three

aunts and to hear their colourful history. I must go back and oversee some more of the confiscations I recently ordered and also conduct a general check for any kester plants." The corpulent creature staggered off coasting, leaving Alice alone with the nickelonian. Alice didn't like the look of the creep, replete with a full repertoire of eccentricities, but on the whole she calculated it would be quite as safe to stay with him as to go after that savage transvestic monarch: so she waited.

The nickel head finally sat up and rubbed his eyes: then he watched Melinda till she was out of sight, at which point he chuckled. "Man, what fu*k*ng fun!" snickered the nickelonian, half to himself, half to Alice.

"What the intercourse is the frigging fun?" inquired an impatient Alice.

"Why, she," informed the nugget muncher and ardent non-toucher. "It's all her fancy, that: they never confiscate the pshytte, you know. Come on!"

"Everybody says 'come on!' here," reflected Alice, as she went slowly after him: "I never was so ordered about in all my f*****g life, not once!"

They had not gone far before they saw the three aunts in the distance, sitting shaking and feenin on a little ledge of rock, and, as they gained them in proximity, Alice could hear them sighing in a most atrabilious manner as if their hearts were on the point of breaking. She pitied them profoundly, picturing them in her mind's eye as a veritable triptych of the living-dead. "What's their f****** problem?" she inquired of the noser, who answered very nearly in the same words as before, "It's all their fancy, that: they haven't got a problem, you know. Come on!"

So they went up to Aunt Mary, Aunt Nora, and Aunt Hazel, who were all dressed in the identical picturesque, if unconventional and anachronistic, habiliments, that made any comparison to the three witches in Shakespeare's Scottish play far stronger than mere plausibility, and all three looked at them with large, dolorous eyes full of tears, but said nothing.

"This here young binger like," explained the nickelonian in quaint, rustic idiom, "like wants to know your hiss-to-ree."

"I'll tell it her," said Aunt Hazel in a deep, hollow, junkie voice: "sit down, both of you, and don't speak a word till I've finished."

So they sat down and all remained speechless for several minutes. Alice reasoned to herself, "I don't see how she can

ever finish, if she doesn't begin." But she waited patiently and temporally alleviated the monotony by freshening up with a line of fast white lady.

"Once," said Aunt Hazel at last, after a pre-linguistic cough and with a deep, junkie sigh, "I was a respectable undercover uncle in Saskatoon."

These words were followed by a very long silence, broken only by an occasional exclamation of "mphhhh!" from the frequent-snorting nose candy man and the constant heavy sobbing of the mightily morose Aunt Mary. Piqued by her discursive incompletion, Alice was on the point of getting up and saying, "Thank you, madam, for your most uninteresting story," but she couldn't help thinking there must be more to come, so she sat still and patiently said nothing.

"When we were little," Aunt Hazel went on at last, more tranquil, though still sobbing intermittently, "we went to school in the inner city. The master was a heavy new jack swinger—we used to call him Maurice (Nora: Mau-riass), but his real name was Ronny—"

"Why did you call him Maurice, if it wasn't his name?" Alice inquired understandably bemused.

"We called him Maurice (Nora: *Mau-riass*) because he gave us *more rice*," said Aunt Hazel seemingly pissed off: "really you are so bone-head dull!"

"You ought to be ashamed of yourself for asking such a simple question," added the nickelonian in sympathetic endorsement; and then they all sat silent and looked at poor Alice, who felt ready to sink into the earth. At last the baby t fiend spoke to Aunt Hazel, "Rock on, sister, with your hist-or-eee! Don't be all day about it!" and she went on in these words:

"No problem. So anyway, we went to school in the inner city, though you mayn't believe it —"

"I never said I didn't!" interrupted Alice impatiently.

"You f*cking well did," demurred the aunt, completing her

sentence with a salvo of unsurpassable malediction.

"Hold your tongue hoe!" added the back to backer, before Alice could speak again. Aunt Hazel had recommenced.

"We had the best of educations—in fact, we went to school every other day—where we traded dope—mainly to young huffers: glueys you know."

"*I've* been to a day-school, too," said a predictably competitive but surprisingly confrontational Alice; "you needn't be so proud as all that."

"With good supplies?" asked the old acid cubist and sometime air blaster, a little querulously, but with genuine curiosity.

"Yep," assured Alice, "we scored baby bhangs and fantasia from a local gang member named Jug Ears—and fast white lady too."

"And kangaroo?" interrogated all three aunts in unison.

"No way! Are you kidding?" replied Alice indignantly.

"Ah! then yours wasn't a really good school," reciprocated Aunt Hazel downing an amyl nitrite with a metaphorical gulp of great relief. "Now at *ours* they had available at the end of the day: kali, rainy day woman, lucy in the sky with diamonds, rasta weed *and* an assortment of uppers, nemmies and utopiates."

"You could have gotten that kind of pschyt anywhere," responded Alice in a most dismissive rejoinder, "living in the inner city."

"But we couldn't afford to score any of it," confessed two of the three aunts with a brace of deep, lugubrious inhalations. "We had to resort to sniffing airplane glue that we boosted from the local ToysЯus store."

"How was that?" inquired Alice, now, as forever, yearning for a new amp.

"As good as it could be," Aunt Mary replied; "and then our pocket money was increased by our kind parents and so we moved on to the different branches of amphetamines—speed, whiz bang, throttle, and other variant racemic sympathomimetic amines."

"I never heard of 'racemic sympathomimetic amines,'" Alice ventured to annex. "What the hell are they when they're in town?"

The cat's pee neanderthal lifted up both his base pipes in surprise. "What! Never heard of racemic sympathomimetic amines!" he exclaimed. "You know what to snort is, I suppose?"

"Obviously, dickhead," retorted Alice aggressively: "it means—to—make—a fine line out of the new addition on a flat surface—using the edge of a credit card or a razor blade, and then you shlook it through the nostril of your choice."

"Well, then," the cabello head continued, "if you don't know what racemic sympathomimetic amines are, you are a frigging simpleton."

Alice was experiencing increasing exasperation and did not feel encouraged to ask any more questions about it, so she turned to Aunt Hazel and inquired, "What else had you to learn, Aunt Hazel?"

"Well, there was freebasing," the extremely jammed aunt retorted, counting off the subjects on her fingers, "—galluping, taking a cruise, hailing with half a football field, g-shooting and half loading, plus cadillac expressing, tango and cashing, not to mention Kansas grassing, rave energizing, b-bombing and waffle dusting—the karachi supplier was an old and ardent karo drinker named Sidney, who used to supply the school twice a week: *He* was a great babysitter and taught us nexus flipping, nickel bagging, how to get snotty, and how to rave without sexstacy."

"What was *that* like?" asked Alice curiously.

"A bit like cunnilingus from the Pope," a giggly, saucy and slightly *scabreux* Aunt Mary interjected: "Pshitte, I'm too fricking gowed up. And the rane head never tried it."

"Hadn't time," admitted the dead road darter between

joy pops: "I went to the head runner, though. He was an old dinosaur, he was, with quite a monkey on his back"

"I never went to him," Aunt Hazel confessed after terminating a protracted junkie cough with some expectorated lime-green phlegm: "although he sold kawaii electric, back-breakers, sandoz, tachas, sleet, a variety of texas sunshines, and the odd sandwich bag of ultimate."

"So he did, so he did," affirmed the cadillac head, wheezing in his turn; and all four bedbugs hid their faces in their hands.

"And how many bags of glue a day did you manage?" asked Alice, in a hurry to change the subject.

"Ten bags the first day," informed Aunt Mary: "nine the next, and so on."

"What a stupid fornicating plan!" exclaimed Alice judgmentally.

"That's the reason they're called sniffing *lessons*," the c-dust habitual remarked: "because the quantity *lessens* from day to day."

Overlooking the very bad pun, this was quite a novel idea in drug education to Alice, and she ruminated upon it a little before she made her next, calculated comeback. "Then the eleventh day must have been a c-dust must?"

"Of course it was," growled the three aunts, almost but not quite in unison.

"And how did you manage on the twelfth?" Alice inquired eagerly.

"That's enough about lessons," the nickelonian interrupted in a very decisive tone: "tell her something about the games now."

CHAPTER X.

The Mobster Quadrille

In a totally wasted, crackhead manner, Aunt Hazel drew the back of her right hand slowly across her eyes. She looked at Alice with avowed incredulity and attempted to speak, but, for a minute or two uncontrollable inertia choked her voice as it struggled through her blistered lips with death-ushering melancholy. "Same as if she had ingested a bad bundle," observed the now truly pegged sleepwalker: and he set to work shaking her and punching her in the back. At last Aunt Hazel violently blew up chunks, gradually recovered her voice, and with small quantities of ultimate festooning her shrivelled upper lip and nostrils, she went on again:

"You may not have spent much time in the inner city—" ("I haven't, thank God," asserted Alice reflecting on her privileged Bishop Strachan education) "and perhaps you were never even introduced to a mobster—" (Alice began to say "I once dated a—" but checked herself hastily, and said "No, way ho zay") "—so you can have no idea what a delightful thing a Mobster Quadrille is!"

"No idea whatsoever," responded Alice with an indisputably honest emphasis. "What sort of a dance is it?"

"Why," interjected the tecatos, "it's a historic dance, fashionable in the late 18th and early 19th centuries in elite Parisian ballrooms, performed by four couples in a rectangular formation, and seems to be a precursor to contemporary square dancing. You first get high on an abe of macaroni and cheese, then form into a line along a graffiti-enhanced wall—"

"Two lines, asshole!" corrected one of the aunts assertively.

"Gangbangers, BGDs, bloodettes, and so on; then, when you've cleared all the geek monsters out of the way—"

"*That* generally takes some time," added the basehead.

"—you crip walk twice—"

"Each with a mobster as a partner!" specified the extremely skied snowbird.

"Of course," Aunt Hazel explained: "you shoot up twice in

quick succession, set to two dead rags—"

"—change mobsters, and retire in the exact same order," continued the thirty-eighter.

"Then, you know," the number three aunt went on, "you throw the—"

"The mobsters!" shouted the white powder aficionado with a super-human leap into the oxygen expanse.

"—as far out of the 'hood as you f**king well can—"

"Chase after the motherf**kers!" screamed the binger as he bogarted another joint.

"And smash into their fu*k*ng fenders!"ululated the insanely high Aunt Nora, capering wildly about in uncontrollable terpsichorean abandon.

"Change mobster's again!" bellowed the blowout monster at the top of his voice.

"Back into the 'hood again, and that's all for the first figure," concluded Aunt Hazel, suddenly dropping her voice; and the two other aunts, who had been jumping about each in the fashion of a rabid banshee all this time, sat down again utterly spaced out and noiselessly squinted at Alice.

"It must be a very pretty cool dance. Does it involve Saturday night specials such as the Raven Arms M-25 or some equally comparable .25 caliber semi-automatic, and hair-raising car chases through shop windows, and on into poor unfortunate market vendors' vegetable stalls set up in Chinatown and up and down steep, narrow streets?" asked Alice excitedly.

"No such luck. Would you like to see a little of it?" queried Aunt Mary.

"Very much indeed, that would be way so cool," proclaimed Alice.

"Come, let's try the first figure again!" suggested Aunt Mary to the top gunner. "We can do without mobsters, you know. Which one shall sing?"

"Oh, *you* sing," drawled the sherm head. "I'm riding the wave right now on some wacky terbacky."

So they commenced with laudable solemnity to dance round and round Alice, every now and then treading on somebody's toes when they passed too close and waving their crack pipes to mark the time, while Aunt Mary sang very slowly and sadly—

Strummm!

"Will you toke a little faster?" said a basehead to a hype.
"There're some a-bombs in the bathroom and a match to light the pipe.
See how eagerly the mobsters and the hookers smoke their pot!
They're not wasted out on reefers—so they need to score a shot."
Will you, won't you, will you, won't you, will you share a toke?
Will you, won't you, will you, won't you, won't you share a toke?

"You can really have no notion how obnoxious we will stammer,
When they nab us and they throw us, with the mobsters, in the slammer!"
But the hype replied "Bad pshit, bad pshit!" then not a word he spoke—
As he mainlined hail, then downed some ale, but would not share a toke.
Would not, could not, would not, could not, would not share a toke.
Would not, could not, would not, could not, could not share a toke.

"What matters it how far we go?" his wasted friend replied.
"There is another score, you know, upon the other side.
The further off from Canada the nearer is to France—
And they've got pot that's really hot to make your brain cells dance."
Will you, won't you, will you, won't you, will you share a toke?
Will you, won't you, will you, won't you, won't you share a toke?

"Thank you, it's a very interesting dance to watch," quipped Alice sarcastically, feeling blissfully relieved that the painful manifestation of choreographic mediocrity was concluded at last, but added with indisputable probity: "and I think that song about sharing a toke is way too cool!"

"Oh, as to the toke," informed Aunt Mary, biting her lips on another amp joint, "they—you've tried doobies, of course?"

"Natch," affirmed Alice in a fiercely competitive manner, "and frequently. I had my first when I was six at a friend's bar mitzvah and I've often scored them at—" she checked herself hastily.

"I don't know where—may be," muttered Aunt Nora through a miasma of jay smoke, "but if you've been acing the afghani indica since you were six, of course you know what they're like."

"Naturally, you dumb asshole," Alice antiphonated venomously. "I roll them in a vega and add a little lady snow; they're the preferred smoke of most mouth workers I know."

"You're wrong about the mouth workers," retorted a disputatious Aunt Mary, opening another penny balloon. "Take it from an old expert, most mouth workers prefer chasing the dragon or batuwhore. But those users *have* their heads up their asses; and the reason is —" here the three now excessively loopy aunties yawned and shut their eyes. "—Tell her about the reason and all that," they pleaded to the crack fiend.

"The reason is and all that," dribbled out the lady snowman, "that they *would* go with the mobsters to the dance. So they got thrown in the slammer, as the song tells you. So they had to hide their goods in a new stash and find a safe place to freshen up while in jail. So they did a kester plant of all the studio fuel and got their heads up in their asses to snort covertly. So they couldn't get them out again. That's all."

"Thank you," responded Alice, marvelling at the stellar logic embedded in the aunt's micronarrative, "it's very interesting. I never knew so much about heads and asses and kester plants before, the latter of which I thought grew in botanical gardens."

"I can tell you more than that, if you like," added the snowman. "Do you know why a packet of heroin's called a cigarette?"

"I haven't the faintest frigging idea," answered Alice with overt honesty. "Why?"

"*Well, cigarettes like to read the paper when they shoot up,*" the powder fiend replied very solemnly, italicizing his words for emphasis.

Alice was puzzled to the max. "Cigarettes like to read the paper when they shoot up!" she repeated with marked incredulity.

"Why, in what sizes do you buy your pshytte?" asked the blowcaine tweak. "I mean, what dimensions make it conveniently portable?"

Alice looked down at her balloon with orchestrated deliberation and considered a little before she tendered her answer. "Dance fever and decadence are the easiest to score by the abe," the c head continued knowingly in a deepening voice, "from inner-city runners. Now you know."

"And is it pure, you know—the genuine thing?" Alice inquired in a spirit of authentic curiosity. "The decadence is straight madman, you know: methylenedioxymethamphetamine, it's much easier to ingest than pronounce. The dealers manufacture it in their own labs out in Sault Ste. Marie and Halifax; the dance fever's uncut fentanyl, of course," the crackersaurus replied rather impatiently: "any dabbler could have told you that."

"If I'd been that hype," uttered Alice, whose thoughts were still running on the song, "I'd have said to the basehead, 'Get the fornication off: we don't want scum bags like you with us serious bros!'"

"They were obliged to have him with them," Aunt Hazel intelligently informed: "no wise darter would go anywhere without some lighter backup. Besides, he was the chief judge's son and helped them out by body-bagging and kester planting as well as body-stuffing."

"No kid," remarked Alice with an air of ambient surprise.

"Of course not, dickhead," demurred the aunt: "why, if a dealer came to *me*, and told me he was waiting for a kilo of dead on arrival to arrive, I should ask 'By which root?'"

"Don't you mean 'route'?" queried Alice.

"I mean what I f**king well say," Aunt Mary retorted in an indubitably offended and incontrovertibly pragmatic manner, toking her roach down to its final two millimetres on a jefferson airplane. And the c head added "Come, let's hear some of *your* adventures."

"I could tell you my adventures—beginning from this morning," informed Alice a little timidly: "but it's no use going back to yesterday, I'm much too fried for that. Besides I was a different person then."

"Explain all that," demanded the three aunts in choric unison.

"No, no! The adventures first," demanded the florida snowman with an air of palpable impatience: "explanations are such a drag."

So Alice, the dear little uninhibited, schizophrenic junkhead, began recounting her adventures from the time she first saw the young-teller-with-shocking-pink-hair-turned-electric-green-and-now-known-to-be-a-bag-bitch-called-Samantha, and pursued her down the Tronna man-hole with the full intention of mugging her. She was somewhat trepidatious about the matter at first, the three wise monkeys got so close to her, one on each side and one behind her, and opened their eyes and mouths so *very* wide with their jaws frozen in cataleptic suspension, but she gained in both courage and fortitude as she progressed. Despite the fact that her listeners were by now experiencing coke bugs on their skin, they all remained perfectly tranquil and attentive till she got to the part about her repeating *You are stoned, Father William,* to the emaciated Chronic dressed in the coarse green pelisse with the waist an inch beneath the armpits and the words all coming out different, and then Aunt Mary drew a long deep toke on her p-dog, before commenting "That's very freaking curious."

"It's all about as frigging curious as it can be," assessed the wired dragon chaser.

"It all came out different!" Aunt Hazel reiterated reflectively after getting snotty once more. "A sort of lyrical bad bundle. I should like to hear her try and repeat something now. Instruct her to commence." She looked at the kangaroo technician as if she thought he exercised some kind of authority over Alice.

"Stand up and repeat '*Tis the Voice of the Buffer*,'" demanded the boubou head.

"How those fornicated-up junkies order me about, and make me repeat corny lyrics!" thought Alice; "I might as well be on freeking American Idol in front of Paula Abdul and Simon Cowell." However, she elevated herself with consummate dignity and began to reiterate obediently, but her head was so full of the Mobster Quadrille, that she hardly knew what the intercourse she was saying, and the words came out like really weird—

Strummm!

"Tis the voice of the buffer; I heard him declare,
'You have baked me too brown, I must cocaine my hair.'
As a hoe up her asshole, so me up my nose
Snort my beautiful boulders and jab in my toes."

"When supplies have run out, and my pimp has no more,
I will go on a mission to score me some more,
But, when supply rises and batches abound,
I'll jack-up with Big H and pass pshit around."

"That's different from what I used to say when I was a child beat artist," quoth the bebe bedbug.

"Well, we've never heard it before," confessed Aunts Mary, Nora, and Hazel sequentially, "but it sounds uncommon junk-inspired bullshit to us."

Alice emitted nothing in response beyond a silent fart; she had sat down with her face looking down to her hands as she tried to roll another maconha, wondering if anything would ever happen in a natural way again.

"I should like to have it explained," informed the freshly re-stoned Aunt Mary.

"She can't explain it," added the beemerphile hastily. "Go on with the next verse."

"But about his toes?" the chaser catechized. "How could he snort boulders and jack-up in his toes without falling over?"

"It's the very first principle in acrobatically inspired shebanging," Alice happily informed, but was dreadfully puzzled by the whole thing and longed to change the subject.

"Get the feces on with the next verse," the cokehead commanded impatiently: "it begins 'I passed by his c joint.'"

Alice didn't dare to disobey, though she felt sure it would all come out most erroneously as before, and she recommenced in a trembling voice that clearly lacked confidence—

Strummm!

I passed by his c joint, while munching a snack,
While the hoe and the buffer were sharing some crack—
The buffer balled c-dust, and buda and buds,
While the hoe just had cat's pee as her share of the goods.
When the goods were all finished, the hoe, as a boon,
Was kindly permitted to pocket the spoon:
While the buffer received pipe and crumbs with a growl,
And concluded the party—

"What is the frigging use of repeating all that dumb-ass garbage," the three mystic apes interrupted *a capella*, "if you don't explain it as you go on? It's by far the most confusing pshit we've ever heard!"

"Yes, I think you'd better leave off," advised the candy flipping joy popper, recovering from a temporary overdose: and Alice was only too glad to oblige.

"Shall we try another figure of the Mobster Quadrille?" the quartz meister went on. "Or would you like one of the aunties to sing you a song?"

"Oh, a song, please, if Aunt Nora would be so kind," Alice replied so eagerly that the poison person opined, in a rather offended tone, "Hm! No accounting for tastes! Sing her '*Beautiful Schmack*,' will you, old girl?"

Aunt Nora sighed deeply and after a single, extended toke of her superweed (mixed with a little nanoo), began (in a voice sometimes choked with sobs) to sing the following—

Strummm!

"Beautiful Schmack, so grand when seen,
Waiting in a syringe clean!
Who for such dainties would not spend a bit?
Schmack of the evening, beautiful Schmack!
Schmack for your evening, beautiful Schmack!
    Beau—ootiful Schh—mmaack!
    Beau—ootiful Schh—mmaack!
Schhh—mmaack for your e—e—evening,
    Beautiful, beautiful Schmack!

"Beautiful Schmack! Who cares for speed,
Or kiff, to satisfy your need?
Who would not give all else for a bit
Of a needle of beautiful Schmack?

A bit of a needle of beautiful Schmack?
Beau—ootiful Schh—mmaack!
Beau—ootiful Schh—mmaack!
Schhh—mmaack for your e—e—evening,
Beautiful, beauti—FUL SCHMACK!"

"Chorus again!" ululated the isometric dames in unison, and Aunt Nora had just begun to repeat it when a cry of "The trial's beginning!" was heard in the distance.

"Get a move on!" cried the thirst monster, and taking Alice by the hand hurried off, without waiting for the end of the song.

"What trial is it?" Alice panted as she ran with inspirational alacrity, but the scrape and snorter only answered "Get a move on!" and augmented his velocitation, while more and more faintly came, carried on the warm breeze that followed them, the melancholy words:—

"Schmm—aacck of the e—e—evening,
Beautiful, beautiful Schmack!"

CHAPTER XI.

Who Stole the Batch?

The King and Queen of Cocaine were seated with their uzis at the ready when they arrived, with a great crowd assembled about them—all sorts of little addicts and runners, as well as the entire gamut of assorted low-life: travel agents, poison people, ticket scalpers, quinolone suppliers, absentee landlords of Bangladeshi clothing factories, coke barons and vice lords, meth makers, unrepentant needle freaks, ex-Tonton Macoute (still loyal to the late Papa Doc), corrupt city mayors and federal ministers, car-jackers, scags seriously up against the stem, fluently bilingual con men, internationally renowned athletes, cyber terrorists, a brace of Mother Superiors, pedophiles, hustlers, and fluff artists: Lenny the Knave was standing before them, in chains and emitting a pronounced aura of despondency, with a gangbanger on each side to guard him; and near the Cardinal stood Samantha with a pony pack of red chicken in one hand and a well-used maserati in the other. In the very middle of the room was a table with a vast assortment of enticements upon it: fat bags, wash, k-blast, loads of r-balls, back dex, kabayo, zigzags of mary weaver, and loads of wedding bells. They all looked so appetizing, that they made Alice quite hungry to partake of some—"I wish they'd get the fu***ng trial over and done with," she meditated, "and hand round the poisons! I desperately need to get shot down!" But there seemed to be zero chance of this, so she lit up her remaining stick of johnson grass and began picking at her scabs and mindlessly looking at everything about her to pass away the time.

Alice had never been in a gangbang court of justice before, but she had read about them in books about the Sicilian Mafia,

and had actually been taken by her mama and papa with her older sister several times to see *The Godfather*, a 1972 award-winning crime film directed by Francis Ford Coppola and produced by Albert S. Ruddy, starring Marlon Brando and Al Pacino and based on the best-selling novel by Mario Puzo, an Italian-American writer born in 1920 to a poor family living in Campania, Italy. She was quite pleased to find that she knew the generic names of nearly every low-life there. "That's a genuine Gang Lord," she said to herself, "because of his dark glasses and cigar." The Gang Lord, by the way, was Cruz who wore his long scarlet cardinal's cassock (regular Vatican issue manufactured in China, size XL) with a huge and heavily masticated crucifix-pipe around his neck, and a wide, ridiculous hat that made it look as if a scarlet UFO had landed on his head (check out Wikipedia, children, if you want to see how ridiculous a cardinal looks)! He did not seem at all copasetic, and it was certainly not becoming of a senior official in the Catholic Church and a heavy player at the Vatican.

"And that's the jury-box, or is it the injury-box" thought the freshly tranquilized Alice, "and those twelve gangbangers," (she was obliged to say "gangbangers," you see, because some of them called each other "bruh" and "bro," both of which are gang slang for a friend or associate, and some were called "bloodettes," which is a gang term for a female member of a gang. "I suppose they are the jurors." She enunciated this last word two or three times over to herself, being rather proud of it: for she thought, and rightly too, that very few little heavy users of her tender age knew the meaning of it at all. However, "jury-men" would have done just as well.

The twelve jurors were all busily jacking-up. "I wonder what they're shooting?" inquired the incurably curious Alice beneath her breath of the crackerjack. "They can't possibly arrive at a rational verdict if they're all-lit-up."

"It's the way it's done around these parts," the crackhead whispered in reply, "for fear they'll develop the agonies before the end of the trial."

"Stupid assholes!" Alice assessed in a loud, vituperative voice, but she stopped abruptly, for Samantha cried out, "Silence in the court!" and the Cardinal put out his cigar on the shaved head of an unfortunate officer of the court, lit a lengthy vega of rainy day woman in its place and inhaled durationally as he looked anxiously round to make out who was talking.

Alice could see, as well as if she were looking over their shoulders, that all the jurors were recently reactivated with quartz and gallup and were busily assembling their rigs in order to channel-swim some additional liquid reindeer dust. She could even make out that one of them needed a babysitter. "A nice muddle their head's will be in before this trial's over!" Alice ruminated while lighting up the remnants of an assassin of youth she had pianoed from the floor.

One of the junkie-jurors had a sharp with a bent pod. This, of course, the fastidious Alice could not tolerate, and accordingly went round the court and got behind him and very soon found an opportunity to take it away. She did it so quickly that the poor little junkie (it was a guy called Clarence, a real dead rag) could not make out at all what had become of it; so, after hunting all about for it, he was obliged to shoot up with a gaffus boosted from an aging raspberry sitting next to him, risking contracting AIDS that way. "Herald, read the accusation!" ordered the Cardinal.

On this the young Samantha blew three blasts on her crack pipe, and then unrolled the parchment scroll, and read as follows—

Strummm!

"*The Queen of Hache, she hid her stash,*
  All on a summer day :
The Knave of Trash, he stole her stash,
  And took it quite away !"

"Consider your verdict," the Cardinal said to the jury.

"Not yet, not yet!" the electric-green-haired teller-skank hastily interrupted. "There's a great deal more verbal protocol to come before that!"

"Call the first witness," commanded Cruz; and Samantha blew another three blasts on the crack pipe, and called out, "First witness!"

The first witness was the acid freak known as the March Hare. He came in with a balloon of nice and easy in one hand and a bag of nemmies in the other. "I beg pardon, your Majesty," he began nervously, "for bringing these goods in, but I was afraid some scab might try and sancocho them."

"You should have found a new stash to hide them in, asshole," advised Cruz retrospectively, fingering his crucifix cum hash pipe. "Where did you have them before?"

The acido sipper looked at the gick monster, who had followed him into the court, arm-in-arm with a mature chick called Lizzie (a heavy gondola and macaroni dinosaur). "Alice's pantyhose, I think it was," he stated.

"Her large, hooker-style purse," affirmed the tail lighter.

"Her underwear," corrected Lizzie as she lit another macaroni roll.

"Write that down," the King charged the jury, and the jury eagerly wrote down all three locations on their black-market Dell M2800 Precision Workstation™ laptops, and then added them up and reduced the answer to Alice's bra and panties.

"Give me that ma'a you've got," the Cardinal demanded of the crackhead.

"It isn't mine," responded the freak.

"Jacked!" exclaimed the King in unadulterated jubilation, turning to the jury, who instantly made a memorandum of the fact.

"I keep it for a friend," the c-duster added by way of explanation; "I've none of my own. I travel the cadillac expressway myself."

Here Melinda put on her spectacles and began staring at the garbage head, who turned pale and fidgeted.

"Give your frigging evidence," petitioned the ecclesiastical *paterfamilias*, "and don't be nervous, or I'll have you executed on the fornicating spot."

This seemed neither to encourage nor placate the witness at all: he kept shifting from one foot to the other in the manner of a medieval Morris dancer or a Burgundian grape crusher working to rule, looking with great disquietude at the Queen, and in his confusion swallowed half of the nemmies and dropped his balloon of nice and easy to the courtroom floor.

Just at this moment, Alice felt a very curious sensation which puzzled her a good deal until she recognized the cause: she had been coasting on some recently pilfered blue velvet and was wired to the max once more ,and thought at first she would get up and leave the court to blow chunks, but on second thoughts she decided to remain where she was as long as she could in a perfectly stationary position.

"I wish you wouldn't scratch those lithium scabs so," said the gondola and macaroni habit, who was sitting adjacent to her. "The flakes of dried blood are getting mixed in with my macon."

"I can't help it," avowed Alice excessively loaded, "I desperately need to use."

"You've no fu***ng right to use here," responded Lizzie reproachfully.

"Don't talk bullshit, you clapped up lot lizard," countered Alice most assertively and exercising once again her great gift for invective: "you know you're frigging wasted too."

"Yes, but I get wasted at a reasonable pace," replied the mafu lover adroitly: "not in that ridiculous fashion." And she arose extremely peevishly and crossed over to the other side of the court.

All this time Melinda had never left off staring at the acid freak, and, just as Lizzie crossed the floor, she said to one of the officers of the court, "Bring me the list of the dealers nailed in the last bust-up!" on which the wretched acid tweak trembled so much that he shook both his shoes off.

"Shoot the pshytte with your evidence, geek," Cruz requisitioned angrily, "or I'll have you dehabituated, whether you're smoked-out or not."

"I'm a poor sleepwalker, your Majesty, who's shot the curb," the fried hare began in a trembling voice, "—and I hadn't begun to relocate my stash, and what with the balloons of nice and easy so susceptible to being tapped—and the consistently low grade of the nemmies—"

"Being tapped of what?" inquired the King with authentic interest.

"It began with a B," the brain-wasted leveret replied.

"Of course 'bags' begins with a B, asshole!" shouted the captious Cardinal. "'Tapping the bags.' Do you take me for an intercoursing cretin? Get the fu*k on with it!"

"I'm a poor man," he continued, "and most balloons get tapped these days—only the crackhead said—"

"Screw you, pshit face!!" the baby user interrupted with maximum antagonism.

"You freaking well did!" responded the month-before-April carrot-munching mammal.

"I deny it!" asserted the Mad Hatter emphatically.

"He denies it," said Cruz: "leave out that part."

"Well, at any rate, Lizzie commented—" the limped-dick geek went on, looking anxiously round to see if she would deny it too: but Lizzie denied nothing, being freshly bombed on some baby bhang.

"After that," continued the ultimate freak, "I cut some more nice and easy—"

"But what did the gondola and macaroni head say?" one wasted juror inquired.

"That I can't remember," answered the chronic baser.

"You *must* remember," demanded the Cardinal, wiping some lady caine from his upper lip, "or I'll have you dehabituated."

The mortified applejacker dropped his nemmies and nice and easy once again and went down on a single knee. "I'm a poor pathetic bazooka boy, your Majesty," he began.

"You're a very poor fricking speaker," added the Cardinal. "No doubt from years of heavy using."

Here one of the gangbangers cheered and was immediately *suppressed* by the officers of the court. (As that is a rather hard word, I will just explain to you how it was done. Three of the officers took a large canvas bag connected by thick rope to an even larger slab of concrete, which was tied up at the mouth of the bag with said thick rope: into this they slipped the gangbanger head-first after they had placed duct tape over his mouth and tied up his hands and feet, and then they all sat upon it smiling.)

"I'm glad I've seen that done," admitted Alice to herself. "I've so often read in the newspapers that at the end of trials 'There were some attempts at applause, which were immediately *suppressed* by the officers of the court,' and I never understood what *suppressed* meant till now. I always thought it a cognate term of *suppository*, but I've not the faintest idea why it's connected to that concrete slab, perhaps it's to prevent the large bag with the man tied up in it from blowing away in a strong wind and seriously injuring the human contents."

"If that's truly all you know about it, you may stand down," continued the King of Cocaine.

"I can't go no lower," elucidated the menial powder head: "I'm prostrate on the floor, as it is."

"Then *sit* the *u*k down," Cruz replied as he powdered his nose with additional lady white.

Here the other gangbanger cheered and he too was *suppressed*.

"Totally great, that finished the dumb-ass gangbangers!" thought Alice. "Now we shall get on better."

"I'd rather finish my nice and easy," admitted the pancake flapper with an anxious look at the Queen, who was reading the list of recently nailed dealers.

"You may split," informed the royal candy caner, and the ed hardy shooter hurriedly left the court without even waiting to pick up his buttons.

"—and just take his freaking head off outside," Melinda added to one of the officers: but the craic pate (as they call them in County Donegal) was way out of sight before the officer could get to the door.

"Call the next witness!" barked el Cardinale.

The next witness was the Duchess's methamphetamine lab cook, named Sheila for some inexplicable reason. She carried the Duchess's cocaine-box in her hand, and Alice guessed what it was, even before she got into the court, by the way the people near the door began sneezing uncontrollably all at once.

"Shoot the pshytte, dick-wad," ordered the Cardinal.

"Up yours, Cruz!" yelled the cook in a surprisingly defiant and bewilderingly bellicose manner.

The Cardinal looked anxiously at Samantha, who said in a low voice, "Your Majesty must cross-examine *this* witness."

"Well, if I must, I guess I must, but pass me another handful of them there trucker pills," Cruz demanded with a detectably intimidated air, and, after mustering some courage, folding his hairy arms and frowning at the cook till his eyes were nearly out of sight, he emitted in a deep voice, "What does the stashed batch contain?"

"Pick me up potion mostly, with some abolics (from a retired veterinarian in Nanaimo), acid cubes, half moon, diesel, delatestryls, loony toons, and loads of vikings," answered Sheila unwillingly.

"Vipers," whispered a stoned Lizzie behind her.

"Collar that gondola and macaroni fiend," the Queen shrieked out. "Behead that f*cked up haircut addict! Turn that lackbay diva Diva out of court! Suppress her! Pinch her! Off with her panties! No, better still, off with her head!"

For some minutes the whole court was in confusion, getting poor, stoned Lizzie turned out and Alice turned on, and, by the time they had settled down again, Sheila the cook had disappeared.

"Never mind! I mean, what the hell!" yodelled Cruz with an alpine air of impeccable insouciance. "Call the next witness." And he appended in an undertone to the Queen,

"Really, Melinda, *you* must cross-examine the next witness. The frustration and ordeal are making my track marks itch!"

Alice observed Samantha as she fumbled over the list, feeling very curious to see what the next witness would be like, "—for they've sweet fanny evidence *yet*," she mumbled to herself as she lit up another kick stick. Imagine her surprise, when Samantha read out, at the top of her whisky, junkie voice, the name "Alice!"

CHAPTER XII.

Alice's Evidence

"Holy fecal dropping!" ejaculated Alice, understandably scared out of her wits, while quite forgetting in the flurry of the moment how wasted she had been over the last few hours, and she sprang to her feet in such a hurry that the careless little binger tipped over the already precarious jury-box with the edge of her maserati, upsetting all the jurymen on to the heads of the crowd below, and there they lay sprawling about, most resembling vast quantities of wet, stoned spaghetti, reminding her very much of a rave she'd been to in the east end of Tronna with a group of spoilt, rich, local e-tards from Rosedale the week before.

"Oh pshit, I beg your pardon!" she exclaimed in a tone of inebriated and embarrassed confusion, and began picking the jury members up again as quickly as she could, for the wild evening with the e-tards kept running through her head and she had a vague sort of idea that they must be collected at once and the tomato sauce removed from them entirely before putting them back into the jury-box each with a handful of e-tarts or else they would die from the agonics.

"The trial cannot proceed," affirmed the Cardinal-King in a long-anticipated, intensely grave, Tuscan accent, "until all the jurymen and -women are back in their proper places—every fricking one of them," he extolled with supreme emphasis, staring penetratingly at Alice as he said so.

Alice looked at the jury-box and saw that in her haste she had deposited the *numero uno* juryman head downwards and the pathetic, fat freak was waving his feet about in a melancholy-to-pathetic way, being quite unable to move his obese torso. She extracted him with exceeding difficulty, but eventually succeeded in repositioning him right way up; "not that it signifies pshyt all," she muttered inwardly to herself; "I should think that asshole of a cabbage head would be quite as much use in the trial equally ass-up as head-up."

As soon as the jury had recovered a little from the shock of being upset at being compared to wet spaghetti and downed their lover's speed, and their Dell M2800 Precision Workstation™ laptops had been retrieved and reunited with them, they set to work very diligently to write out a history of the entire accident, all, that is, except "Puff Phatty," the lead juryman, who seemed too krunked up to do anything but sit with his mouth open, gazing up into the roof of the court and closely resembling a stigmatized Baroque saint in a Bartolomé Esteban Murillo painting circa 1663, riding the wave on an eight ball of new magic.

"What do you know about this business?" the King of

Cocaine inquired of Alice.

"Well, for starts, I know that you're not a genuine king and she's not a real queen; you're a bent Cardinal of the Catholic Church *and* a covert member of the Church of Jesus Christ of Latter-Day Saints *and* main supplier to His Holiness the Pope, and she's in drag and calls herself Melinda, but her real name's Jason. But apart from that: sweet f. a.," informed Alice with factual accuracy and meritorious verbal efficiency.

"Intercourse all *whatever*?" persisted Cruz.

"Fornicate all," said Alice emphatically.

"That's very important," Cruz declared, turning to the jury. They were just beginning to write this down on their boosted Dell M2800 Workstation™ laptops when Samantha interrupted: "*Un*important, your Majesty means, of course," she said in an asuredly respectful junkie drawl but frowning and making faces at him as she spoke.

"Oh, right, thanks Samantha, *un*important, of course, that's exactly what I meant," the Cardinal hastily corrigended after downing some XTC with a significant glass of cheap Paul Masson brandy, and went on to himself in an undertone of Tuscan glossolalia, "important—unimportant—unimportant—important—" as if he were trying which word sounded best to his pathetic, wasted grey cells.

Some of the jury wrote it down "important," and some "unimportant." Alice could see this, as she was near enough to look over their heads at their laptop screens, "but it matters sweet f.a.," she thought to herself.

At this moment the regal dragon chaser, who had been for some time busily writing in his note-book, barfed out "Silencio!" and read out from his book: "Rule Forty-two. *All users more than a mile high to leave the court.*"

Everybody looked at Alice.

"I'm not a mile high," asserted Alice, "just slightly *arrebatao*."

"You f*cking well are a mile high," insisted the Cardinal

accusingly.

"Totally blasted. Nearly two miles high, I would say," Melinda added as if to underwrite Cruz's allegation.

"Well, I shan't go, at any rate," affirmed Alice: "besides, that's not a regular rule from the *Drugster's Conduct Book*: you invented it just now."

"It's the oldest rule in the book," insisted the Vatican tout.

"Then it ought to be Number frigging One," Alice opined with significant truculence.

Cruz turned pale (no doubt a bad reaction to the Paul Masson and the abnormally large quantity of ingested scooby

snacks) and shut his note book hastily. "Consider your verdict, while I leave the courtroom to blow chunks," he requested of the jury in a now low, junkie, trembling Neapolitan accent.

"There's more evidence to come yet, please your Majesty," informed Samantha, jumping up in a great hurry, "this packet of paca lolo has just been picked up."

"What's in it?" inquired Melinda with waxing anticipation.

"I haven't opened it yet," confessed Samantha, "but, let me look, it seems to be full of pakistani blacks and a folded-up letter written by the prisoner to—to somebody."

"It must have been that," continued the freshly post-vomitic Cardinal, "unless it was written to nobody, which isn't usual, you know."

"Who is it directed to?" asked one of the jurymen after having surreptitiously jacked one of the other juror's joints.

"It isn't directed at all," informed the green-haired Samantha; "in fact, there's intercourse-all written on the *outside*." She unfolded the paper as she spoke and added: "It isn't a letter, after all, it's a set of verses."

"Not another fricking poem to read," bemoaned Alice with maximum exasperation.

"Are they in the prisoner's handwriting?" questioned another of the jurymen.

"No, they're not," answered Samantha, "and that's the weirdest thing about it." (The jury all looked puzzled.)

"He must have imitated somebody else's hand," deduced the King with grave profundity. (The jury all brightened up again, except Puff Phatty.)

"Please your Majesty," beseeched Lenny the Knave, "I didn't write it and they can't prove I did—no frigging way: see, there's no name signed at the end."

"If you didn't sign it," explained the Cardinal, "that only makes the matter worse. You must have meant some mischief, or else you'd have signed your name like an honest dickhead."

There was a general clapping of hands at this: it was the first really clever thing the King had said all day.

"That *proves* his guilt," Melinda managed to articulate between potent inhalants.

"It proves eff ay of the sort!" exploded Alice. "Why, you don't even know what the f**k they're about!"

"Read them," commanded the Cocaine Rex.

Samantha carefully stubbed out her panama. "Where shall I begin, please your Majesty?" she inquired.

"Begin at the frigging beginning," Cruz suggested, "and go on till you come to the end: then stop and finish your reefer."

These were the verses the young Samantha read—

Strummm!

"They told me you had been to her,
   And mentioned me to him:
She gave me a good character,
   But said I could not swim.

He sent them word I had not gone
   (We know it to be true):
If she should push the matter on,
   What would become of you?

I gave her one, they gave him two,
   You gave us three or more;
They all returned from him to you,
   Though they were mine before.

If I or she should chance to be
   Involved in this affair,
He trusts to you to set them free,
   Exactly as we were.

My notion was that you had been
   (Before she had the fit)
An obstacle that came between
   Him, and ourselves, and it.

Don't let him know she liked them best,
For this must ever be
A secret, kept from all the rest,
Between yourself and me."

"That's the most important piece of evidence we've heard yet," admitted the Cardinal, rubbing his hands and pouring himself another large snifter of the Paul Masson; "so now let the jury—"

"If any one of them can explain it," interjected Alice with enviable temerity (she had got so lucy in the sky on pac man the last few minutes that she wasn't a bit afraid of interrupting him), "I'll give him a C-note. It's simply a battalion of pronouns ping-ponged from stanza to stanza and I don't believe there's a freaking atom of meaning in it."

The carmelyzed jury all wrote down on their boosted Dell M2800 Precision Workstation™ laptops, "She doesn't believe there's a freaking atom of meaning in it," but none of them attempted to explain the poem.

"If there's no meaning in it," ruminated the Cardinal-King, "then it must be a modernist poem of some kind—perhaps by Gertrude Stein, the famous ex-patriot lesbian-American hashish-muncher and friend of Pablo Picasso who lived in sin in the middle of Paris with her lover Alice Babette Toklas, an emaciated woman and author of a cookbook who's now buried in Père Lachaise necropolis in Paris alongside the aforementioned Gertrude Stein—and *that* saves a pshit load of trouble, you know, as we needn't try to find any meaning in it. And yet, pshytte, I don't know," he went on, spreading out the verses on his knee and cutting himself a line of lady white on the surface of the top page with the edge of his Papal credit card; "I seem to see some meaning in it, after all. "—*said I could not swim*—' you can't swim, can you?" he added, turning to the Knave.

Lenny shook his head forlornly. "Do I look like I can?" he questioned rhetorically. (Which he certainly *currently* could *not*, being entirely wasted on salad.)

"All right, semantically sound so far," averred the Cardinal, and he went on muttering over the verses to himself, translating them into Latin as he went along and feeling like a convincingly analytic Northrop Frye: "'*We know it to be true*—' that's the jury, of course—'*I gave her one, they gave him two*—' why, that must be what 'he' did with some of the goods taken from the stash, you know—"

"But, it goes on '*They all returned from him to you*,'" remarked Alice.

"Why, there they are!" exclaimed Cruz in felicitous amazement, pointing to a serious quantity of satan's secret, a hundred and seventeen debs, a quarter-kilo of galloping horse, and three thousand nickels of new addition back on the table. "Nothing can be clearer than *that*. Then again—'*Before she had this fit*—' you never had fits, my dear, I think?" he asked of the Queen.

"Never! Apart from the jitters when I'm feenin," admitted Melinda with balanced indignation, throwing an inkstand at Puff Phatty for no apparent reason as she spoke. (The unfortunate dumb-ass had left off typing into his laptop with one finger as he found he badly needed to make up, and make up he did with the same white powder that was currently trickling down onto Melinda's upper lip.)

"Then the words don't *fit* you," concluded Cruz, looking round the court with a smile. There was a dead and awkward silence.

"It's a fricking pun, dickheads!" he added in a fit of exasperation, but only the paper boys on account of the ganoobies having settled in laughed, "Let the jury consider their verdict," he yelled, for about the twentieth time that day.

"No, no!" interjected Melinda for exactly the same number

of times. "Sentence first—verdict afterwards."

"What a load of crap!" responded Alice loudly. "The idea of having the sentence first! That's what the Khmer Rouge and Pol Pot …"

"Hold your fu**ing tongue, hoe!" demanded Her Majesty Melinda, turning purple (thanks to a recent dart of diesel).

"Up yours, you fat old tranny!" yelled Alice, seizing this mesothetic moment in the altercation to her clear, strategic advantage.

"Off with her frigging head!" the Queen countered predictably at the top of her voice. Nobody moved.

"Who cares for a frigging junkie drag queen?" howled Alice with a canine ferocity (she was totally loaded again by this time). "You're nothing but an ontological freak, not to mention a dysfunctional, social misfit!"

At the conclusion of this parry of effective stichomythia, the entire crowd rose up into the air and came flying down upon Alice. She emitted a little scream, half of fright and half of anger, and tried to beat them off, then suddenly found herself lying on the bank of a purling stream with her head in the warming lap of her elder sister, who was gently brushing away some dama blanca and hashish brownie crumbs that had attached to Alice's hair, cheeks, chin, and lips.

"Wake up, Alice dear!" urged her sister coaxingly. "Why, what an extended trip you've had! I've been reading the Holy Bible and donating lots of my weekly pocket money to the Salvation Army, UNICEF, and Doctors Without Borders while you were tripping on the Good Lord knows what."

"Oh, I've had such a weird trip!" confided Alice, now more baked than the late Amy Winehouse and the never-ending Sir Mick Jagger combined, and she recounted to her sister as well as she could remember them, all her trials and vicissitudes and all those strange drug-induced adventures of hers and all the illicit recreational drugs she had used and abused that you

have just been reading about. And when she had concluded her account, her sister kissed her tenderly and remarked, "It was a curious trip, dear, certainly: but now run in to your tea, jam, and scones and that delicious clotted cream mama gets from dear old Widow Dombey, and don't forget to read your New Testament, and do say a prayer for poor, deceased grandpapa's and grandmama's souls; it's getting late." So Alice got up and ran off, thinking while she ran, as well she might, what a wonderful and blithe odyssey it had been.

But in her sister's mind Alice stood just as she left her, in the long lineup in the local branch of the BMO, her right hand holding her bank book and her mind analyzing the ratio of income to expenses in her investment-chequing account, with the setting sun behind her shining through the glass, revolving doors, bestowing an aureate glow through the entire financial space and thinking of little Alice and all her wonderful (and enviable) subterranean adventures, till she too began tripping after a fashion, and this was her dream:

First, she dreamed of little Alice herself, and once again the tiny, scarified hands were clasped upon her knee and the dull dilated eyes were looking up into hers—she could hear the pleading tones of her desperate junkie voice begging for a fix and that queer little scraping of her lithium scabs to relieve the irritation—and as the sun went down on her youthful indiscretions and as still as she listened, or seemed to listen, the whole place around her became alive with the wired tweakers who formed the protagonists in her little sister's adventures.

The fumes from potent doobies titillated her nostrils as Samantha, the teller-hoe hurried by—the frightened, nameless junkie (who was actually christened Philip Archibald Rodriguez) splashed his way through the laudanum pool—she could hear the rattle of the crack pipes as the crackhead known as the Mad Hatter and his players shared their never-ending ultimate, and the shrill voice of Queen Melinda ordering off all her unfortunate guests to the dreadful guillotine—once more the pig-like sack of merchandise was sliding off the Duchess's knee, while maseratis and uzis crashed around it, courtesy of the strung-out Sheila—once more the yells of the Acid Freak, the squeaking of the gangbanger's heisted Dell M2800 Precision Workstation™ laptop, the whimpering of the darling pit-bull in the public john and the turf wars between the various vice lords, filled the air, mixed up with the distant sobs of the smoked-out, miserable trio of junkie aunts, obtaining relief only by their sad, sad tears.

So she stood in line, imagining herself tripping with closed eyes, and half believed herself in Plunderland, though she knew she had but to open them again and all would change to that dull, middle-class Victorian reality she was herself a part of in Tronna—the sassafras would only be Weetabix in a bowl of warm milk at breakfast time, the g-rocks healthy, gluten-free President's Choice™ granola bars, the satan's secret her bedside saline spray from Shoppers Drug Mart that kept her nostrils clean and open through the night, and the pool of laudanum caused by Alice's breaking of the bottle would change back to the soothing sound of the pouring of bottled Evian water rippling to the waving of the trees—the rattling crack pipes would change back to the tinkling sound of itinerant ice-cream vendors, and the Queen's coarse bellows and *scabreux* admonitions to the pleasant yodelling of Adolph their neighbour, a gentle, adopted, goitered former alpine shepherd boy—and the sneeze of the acidhead, the whincs of the crackersaurus and all the other queer, drug-induced noises (including Mavis's choking) would change back (she knew) to the confused clamour of the adjacent busy schoolyard—while the cacophonous machinic cantata courtesy of the neighbour's John Deere Residential x300 Select Series Lawn Tractor in the garden next door would take the place again of Aunt Mary's heavy sobs.

Lastly, she pictured to herself how this same little anachronistic, schizophrenic sister of hers would, in the after-time, of necessity, be herself a grown crack-hoe, condemned by her lifestyle to the lifespan of a lemming; and how she would go on benders with her fellow needle freaks and perforce turn tricks up against the walls of alleys and parking lots for $15 a pop (or even less) to support her habit through all her brief yet riper years, the complex and loving heart of her dope fiend days

before the shears of Atropos cut her slender thread to release
her from her mortal coils: and how she would gather about her
other little children and turn them on, first to airplane glue,
then candy flipping, then heroin balloons and joy popping; her
bloodshot junkie eyes forever slit and herself always desperate
to score, perhaps even within the dream of Plunderland of long
ago: and how eventually she would sell them hache to feed their
own, now desperate, insatiable needs and find an inexplicably
sadistic pleasure in all their evening agonies, screaming and
scratching in unbearable withdrawals, remembering her own
child-life and those happy junkie days.

THE END.

Notes & Acknowledgements

Alice in Plunderland is one of a series of works in my "Queering the Classics" project that moves to revise, revision, rethink and repurpose numerous classic or canonic texts. The present book along with a companion Alice text *Alice Through the Working Class* (at this point in manuscript) comprise two Carroll Caprices whose generative method is identical. I applied the law of the "approximate homonym" to genetically mutate the title of the original Carroll text and precipitate a different trajectory of narrative. Thus "Wonderland" becomes "Plunderland" as "Looking Glass" becomes "Working Class." The plot follows the original narrative closely, mutating original characters and incidents but hopefully leaving them detectable as shadows, or palimpsests. This homonymic method is not original. Indeed my three great inspirations were Raymond Roussel's method of text generation outlined posthumously in his "How I Wrote Certain of My Books," fellow-Yorkshireman Richard Bentley's 1732 rescension of Milton's *Paradise Lost* and Jean-Pierre Brisset's brilliant method of text generation through an invented homonymic logic and employed in his two great works *La Science de Dieu* (1909) and *Les origines humaine* (1907). The postulate of the latter is quintessentially pataphysical: that human beings are descended from frogs and provable through a chain of homonyms in French.

An earlier draft of chapter one of *Alice in Plunderland* appeared in the on-line magazine *Eleven Eleven Issue #18.*

Steve McCaffery

Author of around 40 books of poetry and criticism published variously in Canada, England, and the United States, Steve McCaffery was a founding member of the sound poetry ensemble The Four Horsemen, with bpNichol of TRG— (The Toronto Research Group), and a founding theorist of Language Poetry. He has published three previous titles with BookThug: a revised second edition of *Panopticon, The Basho Variations,* and *Every Way Oakly* (homolinguistic translations of Gertrude Stein's *Tender Buttons*), as well as editing the first Canadian edition of Stein's book of that name. He is the two-time recipient of the Gertrude Stein Award for Innovative Writing, and was shortlisted twice for the Governor General's Literary Award for Poetry. He lives and teaches in Buffalo, NY, where he is the David Gray Professor of Poetry and Letters at the State University at Buffalo.

Clelia Scala

A mask and puppet maker, sculptor and collage artist, Clelia Scala's work has appeared on stages and in galleries, shops and television in Canada and the United States. Her work can be found in *I Can Say Interpellation* by Stephen Cain, also published by BookThug.

Colophon

Manufactured as the first edition of *Alice in Plunderland*
in the spring of 2015 by BookThug.

Distributed in Canada by the Literary Press Group
www.lpg.ca

Distributed in the USA by Small Press Distribution
www.spdbooks.org

Shop on line at www.bookthug.ca

Type + design by Jay MillAr
Edited for the press by Malcolm Sutton
Copy edited by Ruth Zuchter